THE GOLDEN RECTANGLE

Also by Gillian Neimark

The Secret Spiral

THE GOLDEN RECTANGLE

GILLIAN NEIMARK

ALADDIN

New York London Toronto Sydney New Delhi

ALADDIN

An imprint of Simon & Schuster Children's Publishing Division
1230 Avenue of the Americas, New York, NY 10020
First Aladdin hardcover edition February 2013
Copyright © 2013 by Jill Neimark
All rights reserved, including the right of reproduction in whole or in part in any form.
ALADDIN is a trademark of Simon & Schuster, Inc., and related logo is a registered
trademark of Simon & Schuster, Inc.
For information about special discounts for bulk purchases, please contact Simon & Schuster
Special Sales at 1-866-506-1949 or business@simonandschuster.com.
The Simon & Schuster Speakers Bureau can bring authors to your live event. For more
information or to book an event contact the Simon & Schuster Speakers Bureau at
1-866-248-3049 or visit our website at www.simonspeakers.com.
Designed by Lisa Vega
The text of this book was set in Manticore.
Manufactured in the United States of America 0113 FFG
2 4 6 8 10 9 7 5 3 1
Library of Congress Cataloging-in-Publication Data
Neimark, Gillian.
The golden rectangle / by Gillian Neimark.
p. cm.
Sequel to: The secret spiral.
Summary: Ten-year-olds Flor Bernoulli, a Brooklyn fashion maven, and Lucy Moon,
a Georgia farm girl, use their very different super powers to combat tiny Square Man,
whose mission is to rid the universe of anything round or curved.
ISBN 978-1-4169-8042-1
[1. Mathematics—Fiction. 2. Space and time—Fiction. 3. Ability—Fiction. 4. Fantasy.] I. Title.
PZ7.N42945Gol 2013
[Fic]—dc23
2012028955
ISBN 978-1-4169-8527-3 (eBook)

We asked for signs

The signs were sent.

—LEONARD COHEN, "ANTHEM"

CONTENTS

THE GOLDEN RECTANGLE

CHAPTER 1

A SNOWY WEDDING

Lucy was late for the snowstorm. It was due to blow in at noon, just in time for her older sister's wedding. Snow would swirl up the steps of their back porch as Nell was gliding out the door in her bridal gown under a blazing Georgia sun. Then Nell would get married and leave their little town of Puddleville to go live with Matt in the big city, forever.

The thought was unbearable. That's why Lucy was sulking in the barn. It was so hot the sun was practically burning a hole in the barn roof. Salty sweat slicked Lucy's short brown hair into a wet cap and dribbled down and stung her eyes. It must be nearly ninety degrees and only eleven a.m. And of course, the snow had already started.

Still, she stayed in the hot barn. She'd been there with

1

Mrs. Chocolate, her pet chicken, for most of the morning. Nobody had even missed her. Television reporters from Atlanta had come early and swarmed the house, with lights and cameras on trolleys. The TV station was doing a special feature on Nell's snowy June wedding. Lucy and Nell's father was personally responsible for the snowstorm. He owned the biggest ice-making plant in America, and his machines would crush 40,000 pounds of ice to turn into snow for the wedding, just the way Nell wanted it. This was going to be a day Puddleville would never forget.

Nell herself was the kind of girl nobody could forget. She was beautiful, with smooth brown hair and gold-flecked eyes. She could cook and sew and do back flips with ease. She was basically perfect, and Lucy adored her. But so did everybody else. And that was the problem.

All morning everybody had ignored Lucy. She had sat at the kitchen table in her cowboy boots and jeans, waiting ever so politely. She was going to stretch the truth a little for the news: "I caught a bunch of deer and pulled their antlers off and then let them go. I rode a baby alligator all the way down the creek to town, got me a Coca-Cola, and rode him back home. And I skinned that poor poisonous rattlesnake and made this bracelet here." Then she would blow on her knuckles and shrug. "That's just one girl's life in Puddleville."

But nobody looked her way. They were all oohing and aahing over Nell. "I might as well be a ghost," Lucy muttered as she slipped out the door.

Lucy Moon was ten years old, four foot two, and nicknamed "Pip," for pipsqueak. She was planning to be a horse rustler. She wasn't sure exactly what a horse rustler did, but she was saving up to buy a big ranch, and as soon as she got it, she was going to be the first pipsqueak in history to go find a bunch of wild horses and tame them.

She lived in a brick house on six acres of land in southern Georgia. Her mom had died in a car accident when Lucy was two months old. Her dad and eighteen-year-old Nell filled her world. And it had been a fine world until Nell fell in love. Suddenly, before Lucy could blink, her sister was engaged. And all anyone could talk about was the wedding and the snow. Then life took an even more horrible turn. Nell decided to sew Lucy a flouncy, frilly, hot pink maid-of-honor dress. "Tie me to a pig and roll me in mud. I won't be caught dead in that dress," she'd tell the chicken. Somehow she didn't have the courage to say the same thing to Nell.

But life has a funny way of turning your worst day into your best, and changing the thing you hate most into your lucky charm. In the end, Lucy owed everything to that dumb pink dress.

It happened like this: Lucy slipped unnoticed into the barn, climbed the ladder to the loft, and hiked herself up the piles of hay. Once she was on top, she dropped easily down a secret opening. This was her hiding place, one she'd made herself. Nobody would ever guess, until maybe next winter when the hay got all used up. She even had a survival kit—a pocketknife, flashlight, jug of water, jar of peanut butter, and her dad's laser thermometer. She loved that laser thermometer. You could point its red beam at anything, and the temperature of that thing would show up on the digital screen.

She lay down. She could hear the machines grinding

the crushed ice, as loud as a million motorcycles, and she knew snow was blowing out of their green hoses. She could hear voices. Laughter.

And then she heard the screen door on the back porch bang open, hitting the railing like it always did.

"Lucy, where are you?" Nell shouted. "If you ran away on my wedding day, I'll never forgive you!"

Lucy felt a little better.

"Matt, hold her dress for me. I know she doesn't want to wear it and that's what this is all about."

Next thing Lucy knew, there were a lot of people crowding into the barn. Not just Nell, but a bunch of cameramen, and her dad, and half the wedding party. They were all shouting and stomping around and calling for Lucy, and then Nell said, "I'm going to hike up my gown and climb right up that ladder. She's in that hay. I know it."

"Darling," Matt said, "that hay is packed way too tight for someone to hide there, even for a pip like Lucy."

"I won't get married without Lucy."

"It looks like you'll have to," Lucy heard a cameraman

say. "Otherwise, all your snow will melt and we'll go home without a news show."

There was a sudden, hushed silence. Then a sniffle. Was Nell crying?

"Lucy!" Nell called finally. "I don't care about the pink dress! Just come to my wedding as you are. Please!"

Then Bill Goldsmith, their next-door neighbor, ran into the barn. "Everybody look at the blizzard Buddy's machines have made! Buddy Moon, you are the King of Ice!"

"My daddy was the one who taught me, and Pa Moon taught him," Lucy heard her father say modestly. And then he added loud and clear, "Folks, I know Lucy, and I know she'll do the right thing. She wouldn't miss her sister's wedding even if the whole world were on fire. She'll show up in the nick of time. So let's get on with the celebration. We're blessed today. Aren't we blessed?"

Buddy had a way with words, simple but strong, and people usually agreed with him. Everyone began to murmur, "We're blessed. Yes, we're blessed."

And then the barn was empty again.

Amazing, thought Lucy. *I'm going to the wedding in my blue jeans. And I'll be on TV! I can't believe it!* She pointed her laser thermometer at the hay. It was then that she noticed a small, shiny object. She moved the red laser beam over it. The digital screen read 86 degrees. She picked up the object. It was warm to the touch, a shiny, old-fashioned copper key with two square teeth at the end. The key fit her hand perfectly.

Hey, this was kind of exciting. She turned it over. On the back were words she could barely pronounce.

"*Divina sectia,*" she said slowly. "Well, that sounds about as pretty as a bucket of rocks. I wonder what it means." She thought for a minute, and decided the key had fallen out of the rafters into her hiding place for a reason. *It might have belonged to my great-great-grandpa. He probably hid it there before he died. It could be the key to a buried safe full of gold I can use to buy my ranch.*

The thought was so wonderful that she nearly laughed with delight. Just in case someone unexpectedly discovered her key and her secret hiding place, she opened the peanut butter jar and shoved the key inside. And then she climbed out of the hayloft and skipped across the now deserted barn, taking the back steps two at a time, banging the kitchen door as loud as she could, and racing across the kitchen to the living room, where she ran smack into her dad.

"Ready for the wedding, Pip?" he said, brushing bits of hay from her shirt.

She hugged him. "Thank you, Daddy."

"For what?"

"For trusting me."

"You deserve to be trusted. Even if you took my thermometer and put it in your secret hay room."

Her mouth dropped open.

"You know about my hiding place?"

He smiled. "How could I not? I made the exact same one when I was a kid. In the same place. And of course, my daddy knew about mine, because he'd made one when he was a kid. Hiding in hay goes back a long way in our family. The other day I worked on your hideout a little, to make it more comfortable. I straightened out the edges and made it quite a bit bigger. Did you notice?"

Lucy flushed deep pink. "Yeah, I was able to lie down and stretch out. I couldn't figure out how it had grown on its own. So does Nell know too?"

"I doubt it. It's just our secret. You're a pip off the old block."

He ruffled her hair. Then he asked, "Are those the jeans you're going to wear to the wedding? Or do you want to put on the ones with holes in the knees?"

She laughed. "No, but I'm gonna get my cowboy hat."

"Come look at the snow first, Lucy," her father said, motioning her to the bay windows in the front of their living room. "It looks even better than I imagined."

She gazed out at a sight she'd never seen in Puddleville, where snow was almost unheard of. Their front porch, the stately steps, and the entire front yard were softly blanketed in billows of white. Her dad had even dusted the rosebushes with snowflakes. It looked exactly like a postcard from some faraway place. Yet across the street, the warm sun shone on green lawns without a speck of snow.

"You made magic, Daddy," said Lucy.

"I did, didn't I? I've got to clear a path now so Matt can carry Nell through the front door and down the steps at the wedding ceremony. So go on and get your cowboy hat and shine your boots."

"I'll shine 'em until they're so bright they blind you!"

He laughed. "It's going to be one fine wedding."

CHAPTER 2

FLOR BERNOULLI GETS GROUNDED

A thousand miles northeast of Lucy Moon's house in Puddleville—in a brownstone apartment in Brooklyn, New York—another ten-year-old girl was cleaning her closet. And what a closet it was. It ran the length of her bedroom, with four sliding doors, and was filled with outfits she'd designed and sewn herself. Each outfit was labeled with the place where she'd first worn it, with a handwritten card pinned to the sleeve: "Judy Blake's Halloween party." "First day of fifth grade." "Paris, the morning I finally met my father."

The outfits were also cataloged on her blog, which simply bore her name, Flor Bernoulli.

Tonight she was putting aside all the clothes she'd

outgrown, to give to her French half sister, Aimée. Flor's father, Jacques Bernoulli, was bringing Aimée over in a week to visit New York for the first time ever. Flor lingered over the outfit she'd worn to Paris last month when she'd flown in a magic hat across the ocean. She smoothed the black pantaloons and cape, thinking back about that fateful trip and how it had changed her life forever. For years she had planned for the day she'd actually go on her own to surprise her dad. She just didn't expect it to happen when she was ten years old.

Her mom and dad had divorced when Flor was only two. Her dad went back to France, and seemed to forget about her. Years passed, and he never once called or wrote. Worse still, her mom clammed up whenever Flor brought up her father, as if the memories were too painful.

But just a month earlier, on an ordinary Wednesday in May, all that had changed. Flor remembered each moment vividly. School had let out, and she'd run over to Dr. Pi's Sky-High Pie Shop—the neighborhood's favorite bakery. Not only were the pies delicious, but they curved in fantastic spiral shapes that rose as high as two feet tall.

But that day was different: Dr. Pi had suddenly confessed to her that he was a wizard from another galaxy. In fact, his pies were not spiral-shaped by accident. He was in charge of the Spiral itself, throughout the whole universe, wherever it showed up, in pies or seashells or sunflowers. He had to guard the cosmic fire that kept the Spiral spinning. Without him, every spiral would cease to exist. And, he told her, he feared that two brothers from another planet had found him hiding on planet Earth and had come to steal the fire.

That very evening the two brothers had shown up at Flor's home. Their names were Mr. It and Mr. Bit. They were desperate to find Dr. Pi's fire, because it was the only thing they knew of that would save Mr. It's life, for he was dying. And as it turned out, Flor was the only one who could really help. The Secret Spiral was part of her destiny. So was the fire. She had learned how to make special magic with that fire, a magic all her own.

Flor shook her head, remembering how, on that fateful

day, she had flown in Dr. Pi's magic hat across the ocean, landing in a lighthouse in France. She remembered how the hat had taken her right to the café on a busy Paris street where her father had breakfast every morning. She remembered waiting, jittery and full of anticipation, for him to walk in. And she was ready to burst into tears all over again when she recalled the most awful moment of her life—seeing her dad, Jacques, walk through that café door with his French wife and his beautiful six-year-old daughter, Aimée. He had a new family. He had truly put her out of his mind. But it had all turned out okay. She and Aimée had gotten along. Her father had felt terrible for taking the easy way out all those years. They'd been in touch ever since, on the computer and phone. Aimée was learning English in school, and once a week she'd call on her own.

Just then Flor's cell phone rang.

"Aimée!" Flor said.

"One week until we came," said Aimée in her halting English.

"Until we come," corrected Flor.

"I am so slippery excited!"

"I'm slippery excited too," said Flor, laughing, "whatever that means."

She talked to her half sister for a few more minutes, and then her mom called her for dinner. They were having a vegetarian meal tonight—a big bowl heaped with spaghetti squash, topped with homemade tomato sauce, and baked potatoes on the side. Her mom liked to fancy herself a "colorful" cook. She had fun with meals, when she wasn't ordering their favorite Chinese takeout.

"So," said her mom. "Dig in to our delicious fake pasta tonight. Anything interesting happen at school or the pie shop today? How is Dr. Pi? He seems to have even more business than ever, now that he and Mrs. Plump have gone into business together."

"Something strange did happen today," said Flor thoughtfully. "It was kind of freaky, actually."

Her mom's fork paused in midair, dripping with yellow tendrils of squash. "Really? What was it?"

"All the pies in the shop went flat. And turned into

rectangles. And so did the toast. You know how Mrs. Plump loves her spiral toast. Well, she was hysterical. Then a wind came up out of nowhere and blew the doors of Dr. Pi's shop wide open. I mean, the wind was so hard the windows were shaking, Mom! And it was raining like crazy, out of nowhere."

Her mom put her fork down. "Oh no. This doesn't sound good at all."

Flor made an instant decision not to tell her mom what had happened next.

"It's okay, Mom."

"Oh, really? It's okay? I don't think so. I want you to know that you are grounded."

"Grounded?" protested Flor. "For what? I didn't do anything wrong!"

"You're grounded to save your life," said her mother firmly. "I have a terrible feeling about what's coming, and I am not letting you go on another adventure across the world and through the Milky Way galaxy fighting evil. You may indeed have superpowers, and it all worked out last time, but I was beside myself with worry. It's just not happening again. Do you understand?"

Flor nodded calmly. "I understand, Mom. And don't worry. That was all that happened. It was weird, so Dr. Pi closed the shop early, and that was that."

No, she certainly wasn't going to tell her mom the rest. How a voice had boomed, seemingly out of nowhere, chanting strangely. She shivered when she remembered the odd chant:

One, two, three, four, nevermore and nevermore!

It was the voice of Square Man. A man who traveled through the universe destroying every circle, curve, and spiral he saw. "He's the true enemy of the Spiral," Dr. Pi had told her that afternoon. "And it looks like he has finally found me."

No, Flor wasn't going to tell her mom any of that at all. And besides, Dr. Pi had told Flor to go home and not to worry.

"It's our destiny," Dr. Pi had whispered as he shooed her out the door. "Just like last time."

She had looked deep into his eyes. He was like an uncle, father, and friend, all rolled into one. And she could tell what he was going to say, and he did say it:

"I can help you, and I will, of course, but it's going to be up to you and—"

"And?" said Flor.

"And Lucy," said Dr. Pi. "She's going to be very important."

"Lucy who?"

"Lucy Moon. You'll be meeting her soon. And I suggest you don't judge her by her looks. She isn't a fashionable city girl like you."

Flor had sighed. "I guess you already took a peek into the future?"

"Just a peek," he admitted.

Then they heard that voice again.

One, two, three, four, nevermore and nevermore! I know your name, your name is Flor!

Flor's mouth had dropped open. The voice boomed on:

Little Flor and Dr. Pi. The time has come for you to die! My angle's right, it's always right!

"Run home for now," Dr. Pi had said, handing her an umbrella. "Check your magic book tonight and you'll know what to do. I'll see you in a few hours. And give your mom a kiss on the cheek for me."

Flor looked at her mom now. She loved her so much, but she couldn't tell her another thing. Grounded or not, she was going to meet up with Dr. Pi tonight.

"I forgot to give you a kiss on the cheek," said Flor.

"A kiss on the cheek?"

"From Dr. Pi. He told me to give you one. You want it now or later?"

"Later will be fine. You're grounded, you understand?"

"I understand."

And with that, they went on eating spaghetti-squash pasta, as if nothing unusual had been said.

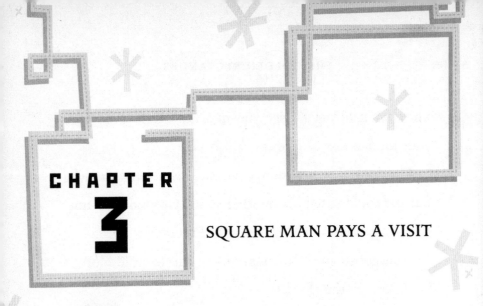

CHAPTER 3

SQUARE MAN PAYS A VISIT

The wedding cake had all been eaten. The television crew had gone home. The snow had long ago melted. Matt had carried Nell over the threshold and off to their honeymoon. Buddy and Lucy sat on the porch swing as the moon rose on this early summer night. Wisteria vines wrapped around the porch timbers, filling the air with sweetness.

"It's just you and me now, Pip," said Buddy.

"What are we gonna do without Nell, Daddy?"

"It's going to be very hard," he admitted.

"We'll be eating cheese sandwiches for dinner," said Lucy.

"That's true. Neither of us can stand to cook, and Nell is practically a self-trained chef."

"And our house is gonna be a mess. Because you hate cleaning as much as I do, Daddy."

"I know," he sighed. "We're going to have to try, though."

After a brief silence Lucy said, "I just can't stand the thought."

"Of what? Missing Nell, or cleaning and cooking?"

She could hear the smile and the gentle tease in his voice.

"All of it. Actually, I don't mind cheese sandwiches a bit, especially with mustard. It's just that Nell and I should have been in a sisters' hall of fame. Don't you think? I mean, we got along so well. I still remember her cheering me on when I fed fish to our baby alligator. She's the one who tied a rope to the oak tree so we could swing out over the sinkhole even when you ordered us not to. She cried and ran away when you shot the rattlesnake, and I had to comfort her."

"Remember when she lip-synched songs using corn on the cob as a microphone?" her dad said.

"Yeah. You built her that little stage."

"She did all of Patsy Cline," her father said. "Then she did Alicia Keys."

"We were up past midnight," Lucy remembered. "She taught me to make sit-upons out of oak leaves in the backyard. We tied the stems together and made a cushion to sit on out back by the creek. Then we brought them in and used them as placemats."

"Actually, it was your mom who taught Nell how to do that when she was young"

"Really?"

"Really."

"She teased me sometimes, though," said Lucy with a frown. "Like when she told me the Spanish moss hanging from the trees out back was actually the hair of witches who had flown by in the night, slept in the trees, and left. But I knew she was teasing, so one night I pulled down some moss and draped it over my head and wore a white sheet and woke her. She practically jumped up to the ceiling she was so scared."

"She believed in ghosts, most definitely," said Buddy.

"Do you think ghosts are real?" asked Lucy, surprised.

"They might be."

"Are you serious? Really?" She was excited. "Have you ever seen one?"

"I have to wonder. Every so often your mother comes and visits me in my dreams, and tells me about things that are going to happen."

"Like what kind of things?"

"She came to me last night, actually, and told me you were about to take on a big challenge. And that I had to watch over you but let you do what you were meant to do and had always been meant to do."

Lucy thought about that for a minute.

"That's kind of weird," she said finally. "I hope it has something to do with horse rustling. I wonder if she'll ever visit me."

"One day she just might. But tonight it's time to turn in for bed, Pip. You've got school tomorrow, remember? And it's nearly nine o'clock."

"Okay, sure," said Lucy, hardly paying attention. She was thinking about ghosts and visits from the dead.

And then she remembered the odd, special key. The

one she'd found in her hayloft and stuck in the peanut butter jar.

"I'll be right up," she said suddenly. "I just have to go get something in the barn."

He nodded. "Yes, you do, don't you?"

"You don't know what it is," she said instantly.

"I guess not."

"Anyway, I forgot it and I'll be right back."

"I'll see you inside in a few minutes, then."

"Catch you in five," she said.

A few minutes later she was in the hayloft, digging her hands into the gooey peanut butter in the dark. She found the key, wiped it clean with her sleeve, slipped it into her pocket, and then began licking peanut butter off her fingers.

Suddenly she heard a voice. "What a wonderful place you've got here," it said.

A ghost, thought Lucy. *I'm being visited by an actual ghost!*

"You like my hiding place?" she said pleasantly.

"In all my travels through the entire galaxy I've never seen anything like this. Why, you've made a perfect golden rectangle out of old hay! The most divine rectangle among rectangles. The rectangle with the most exquisite proportions. The rectangle that can nest infinite rectangles inside itself." The speaker paused, and Lucy could sense disapproval. "It's a bit impertinent of you, though. You do realize I would never authorize dead grass for building such a beautiful thing. Grass simply won't last."

Lucy fumbled for her flashlight and switched it on. In the corner of her hideaway was the ghost, in the shape of an incredibly tiny man about four inches tall. He was wearing a black leather jacket and shiny yellow pants, with a pink bow tie at his neck, and his tiny feet were encased in thick shoes with tightly bound shoelaces. He looked like a cross between a thug, a factory worker, and a dancer in a Las Vegas casino.

The tiny fellow stuck out his hand. She hesitated, then shrugged and offered her pinky. He clasped it enthusiastically.

"I'm Square Man," he said. "I'm the master of rectangles throughout the universe, which includes squares, of course. Squares like myself! Yes, I am very square!"

And he laughed quite a long time, as if he found himself too amusing for words. Then he grew serious.

"Who made this absolutely gorgeous, fantastic rectangle? This very one in which you are sitting and I am standing. It popped up on my intergalactic radar this morning, and I had to pay a visit. Of course, no ten-year-old girl could ever make such a perfect rectangle. I want to know who helped you."

"This is not a rectangle. It's my secret hideaway, but now that you're here, it's not secret any longer. You can have it. You can even have my peanut butter to snack on if you get hungry. Do you have any important messages for me from the other side?"

He seemed confused. "What other side?"

"Well, you're a ghost, aren't you?" she said impatiently. "Daddy said one might visit me and here you are."

"I'm no ghost," the little man said, offended. "I'm the future master of the entire universe! A universe that is turning to squares and rectangles even as I speak."

"Huh?" Lucy shook her head. "Look, it's nice of a real, genuine ghost to visit me, but if you don't have any special message for me, I've got to go to bed."

But when she tried to stand up, she bumped her head.

"What was that?" she muttered, and tried to stand up again, but this time she banged her shoulder.

"I told you I'm the master of rectangles," said the teeny man. "I just packed an invisible rectangle into that opening to close it. Now answer me, please. Who helped you build this rectangle of hay?"

Lucy did not like this ghost at all.

"Nobody," she said.

"Somebody," he insisted.

"Me, myself, and I."

"That's not very funny."

"I wasn't trying to be funny."

"What is his name?"

"What is whose name?"

"The man who built this."

"My dad helped me a little," Lucy finally admitted. "He said he'd made the same hiding place when he was a kid. So he made it nicer and bigger for me. If that's what you mean."

Square Man jumped onto her knee. He seemed wildly excited. Lucy was about to swat him off, but he jumped to her other knee.

"He's just the man I need! Where is he?"

"Inside our house, getting ready for bed, like I should be doing."

"Take me to him now! I need someone to make lots of golden rectangles," said Square Man. "And I'll pay him well. Dollar bills are rectangles, so I rule them, too. They'll just fly into his pockets. He'll be the richest man in Puddleville!"

Like a motorized grasshopper, Square Man leaped out of the hideaway. He must have removed that invisible ceiling she'd bumped up against.

"Come on!" he exclaimed.

Lucy hauled herself after him.

"I am so lucky I noticed your golden rectangle on my radar this morning," Square Man was saying. "Your father is the answer to my dreams. You see, I am faced with a serious emergency. I need help to defeat Dr. Pi."

"Dr. who?"

"Dr. Pi, an evil wizard whose heart is black with hate."

"Dr. Pie? Is he a pie maker?"

"He pretends to be, no doubt about that. A long, long time ago, he and his friends discovered a special property of the golden rectangle. If you start at the corner of the rectangle and draw a curve, and just keep following that curve around and around, bigger and bigger, that curve turns into a spiral. He wants to ruin all my rectangles. And turn them into circles and spirals!"

He stopped, waiting for her to make an exclamation of heartfelt sympathy.

"I don't understand," said Lucy.

"I think I've mentioned that I am completely square? My hands are square. My face is square. How long do I even have to live before Dr. Pi turns me into some ugly round thing? Do you see now why he's my enemy?"

Lucy was interested in spite of herself. "But how could anyone get rid of all the rectangles? There are rectangles everywhere. Like tables, and Kleenex boxes, fudge brownies, windows and doors and bedrooms and beds. I mean, you can't really hate a rectangle. I don't get it."

Square Man shook his head. "He says nature prefers a curve."

Lucy thought about that for a minute. "I guess most things in nature *are* curved, when you get down to it. Like the moon and sun and trees and . . ."

"Not where I live," Square Man said. "My moon and sun and trees are square as can be. Take me to your father, please. If he truly made this rectangle, he will surely want to join me in my battle."

"What do you think you're going to say to him? You're a four-inch ghost."

"I'm not a ghost."

"If you're not a ghost, then a bullfrog has wings."

Square Man laughed. "Think what you want. And I may be small, but my power is practically infinite. You have no idea what I can do."

With that, he took a flying leap out of the hayloft and landed on his feet somewhere below.

"One, two, three, four, nevermore and nevermore!" she heard him chanting as he left. She could not believe the strength of the voice that came out of that teeny fellow.

She was sure he would wake the whole neighborhood. He went on chanting: "Lines and corners, let's unite! Squares and rectangles, let's go fight! My angle's right, it's always right!"

"Daddy will know what to do," Lucy said to herself as she climbed down the ladder and ran after the tiny man. When she caught up to him, out of breath, he was waiting by the back door, tapping his foot impatiently.

"Open it," he demanded, pointing up to the doorknob.

She did, and he strode across the doorjamb, calling out for her father.

CHAPTER 4

THE PIE SHOP CALAMITY

Flor opened her closet door and reached up to the top shelf. There it was. Just where she'd put it months ago. The magic book. She sat down on the bed, her hands moving slowly over a soft, peeling calfskin cover. The title of the book was long: *The History of the Bernoulli Family from the Seventeenth Century Until Present Times*. It not only told the story of her famous ancestors in Switzerland and France, but it actually recorded events as they happened. The print just appeared on the blank pages. "Present Times" really meant present times.

She'd taped her magic key to the inside cover, and she pulled off the tape now, holding the key in her palm. It looked like the key to an ancient castle door. She turned it over, saying aloud the words engraved on it:

"*Eadem mutata resurgo semperdem.*"

And then she translated the saying. "I shall arise again the same, though changed. Always."

Those were the words that one of her ancestors, Jakob Bernoulli, had carved on his gravestone. It was a saying about the Spiral. The Spiral could be found in everything from seashells to galaxies.

Dr. Pi had explained the saying on the key this way: "The Spiral is unique because it gets bigger and bigger without changing its shape at all. Do you know anything else that can do that? And we are all like that Spiral. Though we change and grow and learn through life, something deep in us remains the same."

Life had certainly changed her. And it looked like life was about to change her again. And yet Dr. Pi was right—she was still the same Flor Bernoulli, a ten-year-old Brooklyn girl whose dream was to be a fashion designer.

"Dr. Pi told me to look in the book, and I'd know what to do," she said aloud now. "So let's see what clues my future holds."

She pasted the key back into the book and opened to the last chapter. It had been a while since she'd looked in the magic book, and she had some catching up to do.

"There is a cosmic fire of life," she read. "And it moves and brings alive all the things of this universe. Stars and trees, butterflies and flowers, birds and lions and tigers and grasshoppers and humans, rivers and mountains, everything alive has a fire within. Flor Bernoulli learned how to channel this fire. She followed the directions written on a scroll that was hidden in a magic key and was able to bring a dead man back to life."

Flor looked up. Yes, the book was right. She had breathed life into Mr. Bit after he died, and he had come alive again. Her heart was beating so fast. Did she really want to know the rest? She looked down and began to read once more.

"Dr. Pi was guardian of the Secret Spiral, and for centuries it was safe under his careful watch. But out in the far reaches of the universe, his enemy planned the day he would destroy Dr. Pi, and destroy every last spiral that existed. His name was Square Man. He was made of nothing but squares. His eyes, his hands, his legs, even the heart that beat inside him, all were square."

She shivered. Square Man sounded truly creepy. She went on reading.

"Square Man had great power, though he had not come by that power honestly. He had stolen it. Once upon a time there was a place known as the Beginning of all Beginnings. Therein were points. And the points multiplied, and fell all in a row like beads on a wire. And they became lines. And the lines flowed forward. Some lines curved. They curved until they met themselves again and became circles. Some lines stopped at a length they liked, and met up with other lines and joined together. They became triangles, or rectangles, or squares, or five- and six-pointed stars. Some lines became beautiful golden rectangles. Golden rectangles gave birth to forever-curving lines known as spirals.

"Then the shapes went forth and multiplied on planets everywhere. But on one planet, in one house, in one room, something went wrong. It was a lovely planet, round as a glowing glass globe, and everyone in it was soft and curved and cuddly. But then a little boy was born, and he was not round at all. He was square. He was a square that had lost its way. He should have gone to a planet like Earth, where every shape is welcome. Or he could have gone to a planet of rectangles. But he went to a round planet. And they did not want him. They found him very amusing. They laughed and laughed whenever they saw him. They thought he was so funny-looking. Finally they sent him back to the Beginning of all Beginnings, with a note that he should be delivered elsewhere, to a place where he fit in. But when he arrived there, nobody could decide where to send him. The points argued and argued. And while they were arguing, Square Man saw a beautiful line lying on the floor. He could not quite say why it seemed so beautiful to him. He picked it up. And while they were arguing, he left. He had stolen a very powerful wand. It could pull a circle apart and turn it back into a line. It could take a spiral and unwind it into a rectangle. It could take a line and explode it back into points. Once he learned what the wand could do, he was unstoppable. And he decided he did not want to be sent to another planet. He did not ever want to be laughed at again. 'I will turn the entire universe into squares with this special wand,' he said to himself. 'And I'll start with that planet over there. That will be my home. I will call it Planet Square.'"

Just then Flor's mother knocked on her door. Hastily Flor shoved the book under her pillow and lay down, pulling her quilt up around her shoulders. Her mother opened the door.

Flor rubbed her eyes and said sleepily, "I know, I'm grounded."

Her mother nodded, satisfied.

"I'll see you tomorrow, darling. I'm going to watch some old movies on television."

Flor yawned.

Her mother shut the door, and Flor listened as her mom walked down the long hallway of their railroad apartment, to the living room at the other end. Then she quickly pulled the book out. But she skipped ahead to the final page, where the last paragraph read:

"When Square Man first arrived on planet Earth, he

decided to give Dr. Pi a special greeting. Nobody saw him walk into the bakery, because he was so small. He just trotted in behind an older, married couple. And he sat in the corner watching the hustle and bustle. He listened to the customers 'ooh' and 'aah' over the spiral pies. He heard them moan and groan with delight when they tasted the buttery crust and warm fruit filling. He held his magic wand, ready for the right moment. And the right moment came just when Flor sat down to eat. Holding a small knob on the wand, he wound it like a fishing reel. He pointed it at one pie after another, winding the knob, as if he were reeling in a fish. He was unwinding the spirals. And all the pies went flat and turned into rectangles. Then he unwound the spiral toast. And then, still sitting in the corner, he laughed out loud, as he chanted his anthem and watched the customers run from the store. Dr. Pi didn't even see him as he left.

"'I'll be back,' he proclaimed, though nobody heard. 'But first I need to check out this golden rectangle of hay. So it's off to Puddleville for a day.'"

"Puddleville?" said Flor out loud. "Where the heck is that?"

Just then there was a tap at the window. Flor went over and was astonished to see that Dr. Pi had arrived on her fire escape.

CHAPTER 5

KIDNAPPED!

"**H**urry," he said as she lifted the window and he half climbed, half rolled himself into her room, and dusted himself off. "Square Man is coming for us."

Flor shook her head. "The magic book said he was going to Puddleville."

"Exactly. Puddleville, Georgia. That's where Lucy Moon lives," said Dr. Pi. "But he's not staying long. I'm glad you've been reading your book. Where's the special key?"

"Right here."

"Good. I knew I could trust you." He hesitated. "Put the book and key inside that white purse on your dresser, why don't you? And keep the purse in your hands. Don't let it go."

"Okay." Flor did as he suggested. "Lucy is the girl you said would help us?"

"Yes." He paused. "Do you remember the day when you were in the back of my pie shop after it closed, and the bell rang? And I told you a girl named Lucy had come by, and asked for a pie for her dad?"

"Vaguely," said Flor, though she didn't really.

"I kind of stretched the truth," he said sheepishly. "One day she's going to ask for a pie for her dad. But it hasn't happened yet."

"So you've known all along that Square Man was coming, and this girl Lucy was going to help us fight him?"

He nodded. "But I couldn't tell you, could I?"

She sighed. "No, I guess not. That would spoil the whole adventure, right?"

"Besides," he said, "I only see possibilities. You know that. The future is not set in stone. You could tell me you're staying home tonight, just curling up under your quilt and letting Lucy fight off Square Man on her own."

She laughed. "And you could quit making pies tomorrow."

Suddenly there was a crash in the closet. Flor grabbed Dr. Pi's arm, heart pounding. And then a voice burst out as the door swung open.

"Gad night a livin'! Where am I? Okay, I admit, I did play with that key and do what it said to do, but what kind of silly key is it, if all it can do is plop me down in a closet? And this isn't even my closet. Where in fool's gold am I?"

She was a small girl about Flor's age. She had short, spiky hair. She was wearing a sleeveless blue cotton shirt, faded blue jeans, and cowboy boots. The boots were fantastic, made of embossed leather with silver spurs at the heels. And they gave the girl a kind of swagger.

"Where did you get those boots?" Flor asked, unable to help herself.

"A better question is, who are *you*?"

"Sorry," said Flor, sticking out her hand. "I expect you're Lucy Moon. I'm Flor Bernoulli." She looked over to Dr. Pi, who nodded, and she looked back at Lucy, whose hand was on her hip, and whose brow was furrowed with suspicion. "We're supposed to do great things together," added Flor lamely.

"Well, I'm obviously not in Puddleville," said Lucy, looking out the window to the glittering cityscape.

"You're in New York City," said Dr. Pi. "In a borough called Brooklyn. You are in a brownstone right by the river."

"A river? Do you have alligators here?"

"No alligators," said Dr. Pi, smiling.

"Well, we have 'em in Puddleville. And I ride them to the store to get me a Coca-Cola."

"That sounds like good training for a future horse rustler," said Dr. Pi.

Lucy's mouth opened, then shut, then opened again. Finally she stammered, "How do you know what I'm gonna be?"

"That's a long story," said Dr. Pi. "It involves spirals and squares, girls and magic, fire and a bit of math. Why don't you sit down and relax, and we'll explain it all to you."

Lucy tilted her head and stared at Dr. Pi. "Spirals and squares?" she asked.

He nodded.

"Are you an evil wizard?" she asked.

"I am most definitely a wizard," said Dr. Pi, "but I try to be good."

"Square Man said you were trying to destroy him and every square in the universe."

"That's not true!" Flor exclaimed. "Dr. Pi is the kindest, funniest, best pie maker and wizard anybody could ever meet. Square Man is a liar!"

"How do I know who's the liar?" Lucy retorted.

"Well, you might look at what just happened," said Dr. Pi. "For instance, how did you get here?"

"My key," she said, shoving her hand into a pocket and bringing it out. "I have this key, and it probably opens a box full of buried treasure somewhere in my yard. I'm sure of that. Anyway, I unscrewed the top, and this little scroll fell out, and it told me to say these funny words over and over, while walking in the shape of a rectangle over and over, so I did."

"The magic key sent you here," Dr. Pi said, "because it is part of your destiny to help us. And I believe the key rescued you from Square Man in the nick of time, before he kidnapped you—right?"

"How did you know that? You really are a wizard, then," Lucy said. She plopped down on Flor's bed as if it were her own. "I'm really gonna be a horse rustler like you said?"

"If you want to," Dr. Pi answered. "I expect you can do just about anything if you set your mind to it."

"So tell us about Square Man," Flor urged.

Lucy told them all she knew, about how he had found her in her hiding place in the barn, and demanded she take him to her father. "It's funny, but my dad kind of acted like he expected him. He didn't seem surprised to meet this four-inch ghost at all. And Square Man was actually really polite with him. But then he got mad because Dad refused to cooperate."

"What did he want him to do?" asked Flor.

"Help him fight Dr. Pi and build lots and lots of rectangles together," Lucy said. "He told my dad if he wouldn't do that, he would just kidnap me and hold me for ransom. So I ran back into the barn and turned that key every which way and pulled and pushed until suddenly it came apart, and that tiny scroll fell out, and I unrolled it and read the directions and did exactly what it said. Because he had just found me and was about to kidnap me for sure!"

"Let me see the key," said Flor. "Is it like this one?"

And she held hers out. Flor's hand was delicate and slender with hot pink nail polish. Lucy's small, strong hand was tanned from the sun. Two girls' hands could not have looked more different. But the keys that lay in both looked the same.

"Very curious," said Dr. Pi. "If they don't fit the same lock, then they were certainly made by the same locksmith!"

"All I know is Square Man was hopping up and down and mad as could be since while I was doing this, he couldn't touch me. It was like a big barrier went up. I was totally protected. And then I fell." She stopped and looked at Flor accusingly. "I fell into *your* closet!"

"It's not my fault!" exclaimed Flor.

Lucy shrugged. "I guess not. So what does your key do?"

Flor hesitated. How could she explain it in just a few

words? "It allows me to breathe fire into dead people, and bring them back to life," she said.

Lucy's eyes widened. "That's pretty cool. Want to trade?"

Flor laughed and shook her head.

"You can't really trade," said Dr. Pi. "Each of you has the key that is meant just for you. And Flor's fire does more than she knows. She just hasn't learned everything her key can teach her. The same is true of your key, Lucy."

Both girls were quiet, thinking that one over.

"I guess now that I have this key, nobody will call me Pipsqueak any longer," said Lucy. "They'll be mighty impressed."

"Pipsqueak?" Flor echoed, and giggled.

"Yes, Miss Hot Pinkie," said Lucy.

"Miss Hot Pinkie?"

"Those fingernails," said Lucy. She shook her head. "I guess you're one of those popular girls at school."

"Girls," chided Dr. Pi.

Just then another crash came from the closet, and Lucy's father tumbled out the door, tangled up in one of Flor's party dresses.

"Daddy!" exclaimed Lucy. "How did you get here?"

Buddy Moon stood up, the spangled dress wrapped around one leg and both feet. He stood there, hesitant to move and rip the dress.

"It wasn't easy, Pip. But I'm your father and so I had to follow you, and somehow I managed. However, I couldn't take a direct route like you did, so Square Man saw me ahead of him the entire way, and he's not a few minutes behind me. Meanwhile, I'm very sorry about the dress," he said to Flor, reaching down to gently disentangle the material from his feet.

"That's okay," she said, taking it from him and shutting the closet door. "I can fix it in no time. So you're Lucy's dad?"

"Yes, Buddy Moon." He nodded, then went up to Dr. Pi and stuck out his hand.

"Pleased to meet you at last," said Buddy. "Having heard about you for . . . oh . . . since I was a child, actually."

Dr. Pi smiled. "I remember your great-great-grandfather. We had a lovely chat together once."

"What do you mean you talked to his great-great-granddad?" asked Flor. "He lives in Puddleville. You live in Brooklyn. When have you ever been in Puddleville?"

"Never," said Dr. Pi. "I met his great-great-grandfather on a trip to outer space once. He was guardian of the Golden Rectangle, and I was guardian of the Spiral. I decided to make spiral pies on planet Earth, and he decided to make blocks of ice in the shape of golden rectangles down here as well. In that way we could offer a service to others, and remain cosmic guardians as well."

"You mean all those ice blocks are . . . just a cover?" asked Lucy.

"No, not at all, Pip," said Buddy. "You've seen the big trucks come for ice blocks to keep vegetables cool as they travel across country. And you know that a century ago, when nobody had freezers, ice blocks were delivered to every home at least once a week. They'd put them in a cellar to keep things cold."

"Well, I'll just be darned. Are you a wizard too, though?" asked Lucy.

Buddy smiled. "Not exactly."

Just then there was a rustle in the closet. The door eased open a crack and out slid Square Man, holding a small gold box in his hands.

"Well, look what just crawled out of my closet. Who are you?" asked Flor, staring at the tiny man.

"I'm who you think I am."

"You're all of four inches tall!"

And she began to giggle.

"You won't be laughing for long," said Square Man with a shrug, and he strode up to Lucy.

A TRIP IN A GOLDEN
ROCKET SHIP

So, Miss Lucy," said Square Man, looking around Flor's bedroom, "you escaped me. But you won't escape again. One, two, three, four . . ."

And he snapped his fingers. Lucy looked around her. Nothing had happened. Nothing had changed.

"Go on, Lucy," said Square Man. "Walk over to your new best friend, Flor."

"I won't, just because you said I should," Lucy said automatically. Tentatively, though, she stuck out her hand, and sure enough, it met a barrier. She glared at the little man. "You slapped one of those invisible rectangles on me again. Like in the hayloft. Didn't you?"

He smiled. "One on all sides, to be exact. You are at this moment in a prison of my own design. A rectangular

51

one, of course. It starts at the floor and goes up to the ceiling. Your key won't help you now."

"What do I care? I'm fine in here. Finer than a frog hair split four ways!"

He turned to Flor. "One, two, three, four . . . ," he said, snapping his fingers. "Now you, Dr. Pi. One, two, three, four . . . And you, Mr. Buddy Moon. You could have been my friend and partner, but it looks like you've gone to the dark side, so I have no choice."

"I just disagree with you, that's all," Buddy said calmly. "Rectangles have a place in this universe. The golden rectangle is very special, and a spiral can be spun from it. Like a caterpillar turns into a butterfly. Both have a place, and they rest in balance."

"Beautifully said," Dr. Pi commented.

"We might say that ice and snow are different, but they are both made of water," Buddy went on. "Every day at my plant we turn water into ice."

Dr. Pi nodded. "So here we are with Square Man, who wants to unravel all the spirals and fill the world with rectangles. Why would we want to live in a world without both?"

"Then why did they laugh at me on Planet Round?" Square Man answered. "They pointed fingers and laughed so hard, tears were coming out of their eyes. Flor here just laughed at me. Why is that? Because she is a few feet tall, and I am a few inches tall? Is that a reason to laugh at me? I had no place there and apparently I don't here, either," said Square Man. "You are living in a fairy tale, a fantasy, if you think the world is fair, Buddy Moon."

"I shouldn't have laughed at you," said Flor.

"You're just saying that because I've got you trapped."

She couldn't think of an answer to that.

He surveyed his four prisoners. Then he leaped up onto Flor's dresser and began to pace back and forth, still holding his golden box. He stopped near a neatly arranged column of silver bracelets and gave them a little kick.

"Round things," he muttered. "More round things."

They tumbled across the dresser, and some fell and rolled across the floor.

"So," he said. "It's time to take a trip. To Planet Square.

Where you will all learn a thing or two. And where, Buddy Moon, you will help me whether you want to or not. By the time we're done, spirals will be a thing of the past. Squares rule! My angle's right! It's always right!"

"Where is Planet Square?" asked Flor.

"Very far from planet Earth. But that doesn't matter. We will travel together in my rocket ship, and be there in no time."

And he set his golden box down on the dresser.

"Are you ready?" he asked them all.

"If that tiny box is a rocket ship," said Lucy, "and you're going to make us climb in, then I am a giant of amazing size! I mean, that thing is knee-high to a grasshopper, it's so small!"

"A spaceship would be useless if it did not fold up for storage," said Square Man. "And you don't understand golden rectangles. Inside every golden rectangle is another golden rectangle. They go on forever. I've just folded up my golden rocket ship, and I shall presently unfold it."

And he took the tiny golden box, jumped to the floor, and tapped it once. It rose up on its side, expanded, and lay down again. He tapped it again, and again, and it grew larger and larger. Now they could see that it gave off its own golden light, like late afternoon sun over a lake.

After about twenty more taps the block of gold almost reached the ceiling. He then tapped three times, and a door slid open. Golden light spilled from the interior.

"Wow," said Flor.

Square Man preened, puffing out his little chest. "I see you are impressed."

"He's an easy mark for praise," Lucy murmured. Then, loud enough to hear, she said, "Let me in. I'm game! I've never seen anything like it."

"Four, three, two, one . . . ," he said, snapping his fingers, and her invisible prison was gone. She walked up to the ship and climbed in.

"Gad night a livin'! Look at this cool screen! I think this here is a picture of the whole universe or something—I mean, I never saw so many stars except when I lie in my tree fort at midnight!"

"She loves it," said Square Man with a grin. He turned to Flor. "Would you like to be next?"

"I don't have much of a choice, do I? But I'd like to take my pocketbook." She motioned to the bed.

Square Man frowned. "Why? Is there something in there I should know about?"

"You see how it matches my outfit?" she asked. "I want to travel in style. That's just me."

Square Man shrugged. "Okay. Four, three, two, one . . . Go get your purse and get in the ship."

She climbed into the rocket ship. The inside was also gold and lit by unseen, warm sunlight. It felt good, like a summer's day. Dr. Pi and Buddy Moon followed. Square Man motioned for them to sit down. The gold door slid shut silently, and he seated himself at the monitor, on a tiny cushion, and pressed a bunch of buttons. Numbers showed up on the screen.

"Planet Square. Three hundred light years away. We get there by traveling through four wormholes. That shouldn't be too hard." He paused, then turned to the girls. "Traveling through a hole in space is kind of weird. You'll feel like you disappeared. And then you're back again."

"Show me Puddleville," said Lucy. "Where is it in comparison to here?"

He pushed a button, and the screen zoomed in on trees and rolling land dotted with small houses. He pushed another button and zoomed in on one house.

"There's your home. You're nine hundred eighty-three miles away from it right now."

He zoomed in on the pond.

"There's your baby alligator."

He zoomed up.

"That's your tree fort. Another golden rectangle."

"I built it for her," said Buddy.

"Naturally," said Square Man. He seemed to be enjoying himself.

"You should see my tree fort sometime," Lucy said to Flor. "I've been meaning to have a slumber party there. Maybe you'll come."

Square Man zoomed over a few blocks.

"And there's your ice plant."

Square Man zoomed in on the plant. Past a KEEP OUT sign. His galactic camera peered inside an enormous room. The floor was made of many rubberlike blocks covering steel containers with ice.

"That ice plant makes how many blocks of ice a day, Mr. Moon?"

"Each steel container has four containers inside it. There are two hundred fifty containers. So that's a thousand blocks. Once we take the ice out, fresh water is poured into the containers, and they're lowered back down and frozen into ice again, over and over, day after day, year after year."

"The proportions are perfect," said Square Man. "A thousand blocks of ice a day—all perfectly rectangular!"

"Zoom in on the other room, the one with tons of bags of crushed ice," said Lucy. "It's over to the right, there. See that, everybody? That's where I go every day after school. And even when it's hot enough to fry an egg on the sidewalk, I wear a winter jacket in there. It's so cold! I'm a super ice-bagger. I put the crushed ice in ten-pound bags and seal 'em. I can bag ice faster than anybody."

"There's something wrong with this picture," said Flor suddenly.

Everybody turned to look at her.

"Mr. Moon," said Flor, "where is Lucy's mom?"

Lucy frowned. "I don't have a mom."

"Everybody has a mom."

"My mom died," Lucy said shortly. "I was two months old. I don't remember. Don't play no violins for me. I have the best dad and sister."

"Wow, I'm sorry." Flor hesitated, then said bravely, "Until recently, I basically didn't have a dad."

Lucy tilted her head and waited. Flor could tell she was curious but didn't want to show it. And then it all came rushing out, how her father had moved to France, about his new family and her new sister, Aimée, about her adventure to meet him.

"That sounds awful," Lucy said.

"Sometimes people just avoid things that are too painful," said Dr. Pi. "I think Flor's father didn't know how to make it right. But she inspired him to start being a real father to her."

"Now he calls me once a week," said Flor. "And they're going to visit later this summer."

Square Man, who had followed both stories closely, was strangely silent, almost brooding.

"I have no idea who my mother or father is," he finally announced. And then he thrust his tiny shoulders back. "Nor do I care! Put on your golden seatbelts. You four are my prisoners, and I am taking you to Planet Square, where we will begin our grand task of turning spirals into rectangles."

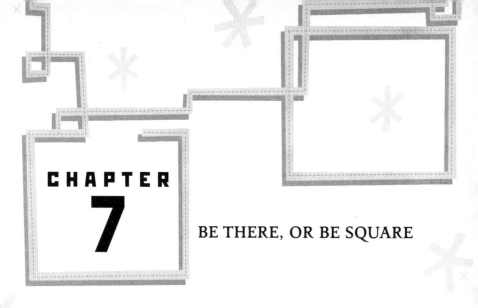

CHAPTER 7

BE THERE, OR BE SQUARE

I never realized how many things in the world are curved," said Flor. She had just stepped out of the golden rocket ship onto Planet Square. The ride had taken only ten minutes, and the wormholes had been no trouble at all. Each time the ship went through one, Flor felt like she was disappearing into nothingness, almost as if she had fallen asleep, but then she reappeared fully awake a few seconds later, and all of her was still there.

Planet Square was brown and gray. The sky was a faded white, like a dirty sheet. Everywhere the eye could see was an endless expanse of rock, made of small squares. It was as if nature had decided to tile the entire planet, and forgot about soil and grass. Every so often a patch of long columns of rock pushed out of the tile, clustered in groups like organ pipes.

Square Man was tapping and folding up the rocket ship. He slipped it into his pocket.

"Lines and angles everywhere," said Buddy. "Amazing."

"A planet without a single curve that I can see," said Dr. Pi thoughtfully.

"I told you," said Square Man impatiently. "Why are you so surprised?"

"But in the natural world, squares are not everywhere. It's easier for nature to make round things. Like raindrops that fall. Or bubbles that float. Or dandelion seeds with their white puffs. Was this planet all square before you arrived? Or did you change it?"

"I made it in my own image," said Square Man.

"What's bumping against my skin?" said Lucy. "Is it square mosquitoes or something?"

"That's wind," said Dr. Pi. "Wind usually flows in waves. But waves are not allowed here. So it has to form rectangles and bounce along."

"And the mist—is that mist?" asked Flor, squinting.

"It's not rolling over the rocks—it seems to be jumping."

"What is that monster coming toward us?" shrieked Lucy, pointing at the horizon.

They all turned. Something huge was crawling over the drab landscape and galumphing toward them. Sweat dripped from its spotted armor, which on closer look was made of thousands of hard, shell-like scales. The creature had two huge claws with pincers as sharp as razors. Two long antennae twitched against the ground as the creature reached them.

The monster stopped and lifted its claws into the air. And there it remained, unmoving.

"Hello, Red Eye," said Square Man. "Meet my four new friends. Dr. Pi is an evil wizard who is now in my employ. We must strip him of his power to protect spirals. Mr. Buddy Moon is a master rectangle maker, but so far he has resisted doing what he knows he must. This is his daughter, Lucy Pipsqueak. And this is her friend, Flor."

"This is the way we die," whispered Flor.

Dr. Pi walked up to the creature and nodded hello.

"Extraordinary. His eyes are made of nothing but tiny squares, a thousand tiny squares."

Buddy followed. "They're beautiful, actually. Precise beyond all imagining."

"That's a lobster's eye," said Square Man. "Made of thousands of tiny square tubes, with shiny mirrors on the sides. He can practically see behind himself. When I came here and got rid of everything round, I saved him and named him Red Eye. Because of the squares in his eyes. He is my trusted assistant."

"A lobster," said Flor. "Right! He looks just like the ones at the Chinese restaurant, only about a hundred times bigger."

"So does he talk?" asked Lucy. "Lobster, do you talk?"

One claw slowly lifted in the air and came to rest on the ground, and a robotic voice said:

"All four lines are equal."

The lobster cleared his throat.

"A square is a special case of a rectangle, where all four lines are equal."

The lobster cleared his throat one more time.

"Where shall I deliver them, sir?"

"To the square chamber. I'll see you there," said Square Man.

Without a moment's hesitation, the lobster swept the four humans into his claws, delicately closing the pincers, and began to crawl away. Square Man followed, leaping like a grasshopper.

"What is the square chamber?" cried Flor, wriggling and pushing against the pincers.

Lucy piped up. "You wouldn't just make a plain old square chamber. I already know you better than that. It's got some special feature."

"Well, it does have one special feature. It has room enough for four right now. But if I don't like the way things are going, the square is going to get smaller. And then smaller again."

"You're going to crush us?" Flor shouted.

"Squeeze you gently until everybody gets their priorities straight. Squares and angles, let's unite! And is what I want so terrible? I just want to stop Dr. Pi from turning rectangles into spirals."

"He's never touched a rectangle of yours," Flor shot back.

"Every spiral was once a golden rectangle," said Square Man. "And besides, I hate a curve."

"But why?"

"A curve thinks it's more beautiful than a line."

"That's not true."

"Nobody appreciates a square."

"I never heard that," said Flor.

"If you want to insult someone, you say, 'Oh, you're such a square.' Did you ever hear someone say, 'You're just a circle'? Of course not. But squares do all the hard work. Square bricks make buildings steady. Square tables hold food. Square chairs, square rooms, square houses. Squares are the basis of everything. And still, nobody praises a square. They praise the sun and the moon and everything round."

Square Man waited for the girls to agree with him, but they seemed unconvinced.

"Everyone should live in a square world. Maybe people will appreciate me then."

Red Eye stopped before a tall building. It towered into the sky, constructed entirely of brilliantly shiny black marble.

"Is this your tree fort?" Lucy joked.

"Ha ha. Red Eye, proceed," he said as a door slid open and they moved inside. Red Eye clattered across the marble floor and through a door, where he finally opened his claws.

"Thank you for being gentle with us, Red Eye," said Dr. Pi. "Those pincers look very sharp, but you didn't hurt us at all."

A lobster can't smile, but Flor could feel a smile coming from the creature.

"What does the world look like to you, Red Eye?" asked Buddy now.

Red Eye seemed to think for a moment. "It was different down in the ocean depths, where it was so dark. My eyes are good for the dark, and I could see well. But on a bright day I am nearly blind sometimes."

Square Man shut the door to the room. Now he turned to Lucy.

"First, I have a few questions."

"Shoot," said Lucy.

"So how did you learn that trick back in the barn when you escaped me?"

"My great-great-granddaddy taught me," she lied, thinking back to what Dr. Pi had said.

Square Man looked nervous. "How is that? Isn't your great-great-granddaddy dead?"

"He came to me in a dream and taught me. The night before you arrived."

Square Man looked at Buddy. "Is this true?"

"Quite possibly," said Buddy.

"Then the famous Buster Moon, the fierce guardian of the Golden Rectangle that everybody talks about, is somehow still around," Square Man muttered to himself. "Not good. Not good." He looked back at Lucy. "What else did he teach you? I'll need to know everything."

"He taught me what the Southern saying really means, when you tell someone you're finer than a frog hair split four ways," Lucy blurted out. *Oh sheesh*, she thought, *why did I just say that? Now he's going to ask me what I meant, and I have no clue. My mouth is bigger than my imagination sometimes.*

"Go on," said Square Man.

"You split a frog hair four ways, and you line up the hairs to form a golden rectangle that is practically invisible. Because, I mean, a frog hair is so fine in the first place, who can see it when it's split? And you can carry the power of the golden rectangle with you wherever you go, right in your pocket."

She could tell Square Man not only believed her, but he was both fascinated and uneasy. Out of the corner of her eye she could see her dad smiling, and Dr. Pi nodding, as if to say, "Well done!"

"When I came to this planet," said Square Man, "half of it was covered with oceans and rivers and lakes. Not unlike your planet Earth. I saw frogs. I got rid of all the water and all the frogs, with their loathsome flowing curves. I never saw a hairy frog in my life."

"The frogs in our pond are disgustingly hairy," said Lucy. "They are covered with slimy hair. It's actually quite gross."

"Is that so?"

"Absolutely," said Lucy.

"Mmm-hmmm. We'll go back there one day, then, and you'll catch me some?"

"I'm not too keen on helping you right now," Lucy said.

"Is that a refusal?"

"For now, yeah."

"I have another question."

"What?"

"How did you manage to teleport yourself to Brooklyn?"

"That part I have no answer to. I have no clue how I ended up in Flor's closet tangled up in all those clothes. I don't even know how Dad followed me there. I'd love to know."

"I'll tell you how," he said. "You and Flor didn't just meet tonight. You have been friends for years. You went straight to Flor and Dr. Pi because you know, and have always known, just as your father knows, that spirals come from rectangles. It's no coincidence that you ran to the two people I came across galaxies to find and stop their spiral-spinning." He shook his head. "You four have been working together for years. How dumb do you think I am?"

"It sounds reasonable, Square Man," said Buddy, "but I can swear to you that Pip never met Flor until an hour ago. And I never laid eyes on Dr. Pi until tonight, though, of course, I've known of him all my life. The force of the universe itself sent my daughter to Brooklyn. Which," Buddy concluded, "presents a far more troubling situation for you. Doesn't it?"

"Or perhaps," murmured Dr. Pi, "Square Man is himself part of a bigger . . ."

He paused. Everybody looked at him and waited.

"A bigger test," concluded Dr. Pi.

"I've never had it easy," said Square Man. "From the moment I was created, I was an outsider. And look at all I've achieved. So I'm not going to worry about that now. Do you girls know the story of Rumplestiltskin?"

"The fairy tale," Lucy said. "Everybody knows that story."

"And what happens in the beginning of that story?"

"A father brags that his daughter can spin straw into

gold, and the king hears the rumor and shuts her up in a tower room with a lot of straw and a spinning wheel. He tells her to spin the straw into gold by morning or she'll be executed."

"Right. So. Dr. Pi. I don't suppose you're willing to give up your obsession with spirals, and let me guide them back to their original form, the golden rectangle?"

Dr. Pi sighed. "You know the answer to that."

"Right. And, Mr. Moon, are you still determined to refuse my offer?"

"I couldn't make you golden rectangles, even if I wanted to," said Buddy. "My task in life is to make sure they are safe and protected. By universal decree I am allowed to make my thousand blocks of ice daily. That's it."

"What about Lucy's hayloft?" demanded Square Man.

"She made it. I just spruced it up."

"Lucy doesn't have to follow those rules, does she?"

Buddy shook his head.

"All right, then, if you won't make me rectangles, your daughter can. The talent runs in the family. And the future lies with our children, so they say."

"That's true," said Dr. Pi. "I could fight you, and Mr. Moon could fight you, and we'd probably win, but that is not our role. It's up to the girls. We can only do our best to support them as they tackle this challenge."

"Well, then. Lucy, I have a proposal."

"Shoot."

"Make me a thousand golden rectangles by tomorrow."

"You only need a thousand?" she said sarcastically.

"One thousand. If you can make a thousand, you can make ten thousand. I'll employ you. Remember, I pay well. You'll be rich." He leaned forward and stared at her intently. "Isn't there something you'd really like to buy?"

"I can't think of anything."

"Of course you can. There is something you're saving up for."

Lucy gulped. "My ranch."

He leaned back. "Right. Your ranch. There you go. You'll be able to buy a very big ranch."

"And a pen for my wild horses," she added.

"Done."

"Really?"

"Really."

"And a lot of cowboy boots," she added.

He waved his hand impatiently. "Anything you want. The money is there. See?"

He snapped his fingers, and dollar bills wafted through the air like snow in a paperweight.

"Hmmm," said Lucy. ""What am I gonna make these rectangles with?"

"Whatever you choose. All I ask is that they are the right proportion. *Divina sectia.*"

"Okay. I'll do it."

He was taken aback. "You really will?"

"Yes, no problem. I will do it as long as I can make them out of water."

She might as well have said she'd make them out of air, or wind.

"Water!" he spluttered.

"Water?" echoed Flor. "How the heck can anybody make a rectangle out of water? The water will just run across the floor."

Square Man grew angry. "There is no extra water here.

Water flows in waves. Waves have curves. Planet Square does not allow curves."

"Then what do you drink?"

He looked even madder. "You are a very frustrating child. From frog hairs to water, I never know what you'll say next. I can't let you have water for rectangles. That's final."

Lucy looked around the marble room.

"That's the only deal I can make."

"Ridiculous."

"It's a simple request."

"Impossible."

"If you can't get me water for my rectangles, why, I'm going to be madder than a hen tied up in a burlap sack all night long. And I'm not gonna make you anything at all."

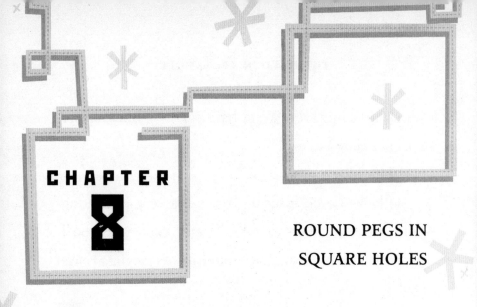

CHAPTER 8

ROUND PEGS IN SQUARE HOLES

Lucy and Flor were trapped. Square Man had decided that with a bit of time Lucy would change her mind and choose a more appropriate substance to manufacture rectangles.

"I am setting my timer," he said. "I am giving you two hours. During that time your wizard and your ice maker will be in the square chamber alone. And it will start to get smaller. Smaller and smaller. I am sure you will change your mind when you think about Dr. Pi and Mr. Moon stuck in a marble room that is slowly shrinking."

"I don't believe you," Lucy lied. "That room doesn't shrink. You're just trying to scare us. So go ahead. No water, no rectangles. That's the deal."

Square Man looked extremely annoyed. "You've seen

the reach of my powers, and you still don't believe me? Fine. Anyway, both you girls can think this over together. It's well known that girls your age rely on each other for everything and get so close you can't possibly make a decision alone. So, Red Eye, take them off, please."

Red Eye carted them off to another room, and when he put them down, they suddenly found themselves standing not on the floor but *in* the floor. More precisely, they were both caught inside square holes about four feet deep. Their feet were fastened to the bottom of the holes, as if by an invisible force field. Their heads and shoulders stuck out—Lucy's just barely.

"I'll be back," said Square Man. "Meanwhile, Red Eye will watch over you with the greatest devotion. Right, Red Eye?"

The lobster nodded and crawled close to the girls.

"We weren't going to try to escape," said Lucy.

"Well, just in case."

"The way I see it, this is *your* time-out, not mine," Lucy said.

"How's that?"

"When you come back, you'll tell me I can make rectangles out of water."

Square Man sighed. "You are truly a determined little girl. See you soon."

And with that, he was gone. After a minute of silence Flor turned to Lucy. "We're stuck. This is hopeless. Dr. Pi's a wizard, but he basically said he's not allowed to help us. It's our adventure."

"Don't worry. My dad will think of something."

"Like what?"

"He can charm the shirt off your back," said Lucy. "And he's super strong. He can tear up railroad tracks with a rubber hammer. He'll just talk his way out of this, and before you know it, he'll be back to rescue us."

Flor rolled her eyes. "Right. Well, until your dad saves us, what do you plan to do?"

"I don't know. I need water."

Flor shook her head. Lucy was clearly a bit stubborn. No use in arguing with her. "Why do you want water anyway?"

Lucy looked around her carefully. "Why do you think?" she whispered.

"I have no idea," Flor whispered back, annoyed.

"When you freeze water," Lucy whispered, "you get ice. Get it? Duh. Like, a thousand blocks of ice a day. . . ."

"Yeah, I get it, really I do, but that's at your dad's ice factory. What can you make here?"

Flor tried to move as best she could, which was just to turn her head, since her body was stuck. But after a while her neck hurt, and there was nothing to look at but a big marble wall, so she turned back. Lucy looked embarrassed.

"I'm sorry," Lucy said. "I just know, somehow I'd make it work."

They were silent. Flor looked around her.

"A square peg in a round hole," she said suddenly. "That's the usual saying. So what's a round peg in a square hole like this one?"

Lucy shook her head. "Don't know."

"Me neither, but it's still a peg that doesn't fit. It means you're a misfit. A rebel. Maybe a bit of a troublemaker."

"We always follow the rules on Planet Square," warned Red Eye.

"Oh," said Flor politely. "I thought you were napping."

"So nobody here ever breaks the rules, lobster?" asked Lucy.

"Everything is uniform," said Red Eye. "Squares are everywhere."

"Why do you serve him anyway, Red Eye?" asked Flor.

The lobster was silent for a long time. Finally he said, "As he told you, he likes my eyes."

"You mean the square tubes inside your eyes?"

The lobster nodded and said haltingly, "And if I leave, Square Man will destroy my eyes and I will be blind."

"Free but blind," sighed Flor. "That's no good. Was this planet always square? Are there other square people on this planet?"

Red Eye bowed his big, scaled head. "There was a Time Before the Square, and now we are in the Time After the Square. In the Time Before the Square, we had water, of course. I lived in the water. We had more water than land. We had never seen a man before, in any shape or size."

"What happened?" said both girls in unison.

"Square Man came and destroyed every thing with a

curve. Every thing that flowed. Every wave. All the water dried up. All the fish died. The trees grew ugly. He let me live because I have special eyes, but I had to become his faithful servant."

"You must miss the water terribly?" asked Flor softly.

"My scales itch and it's hard to sleep."

"You probably feel as dry as an old berry wrinkling up in the sun," Lucy said.

"That sounds about right," said Red Eye.

"I wish I could help you. Get you back to water, where you belong. Down in the deeps, where you can swim all day and your eyes can see like they were meant to. You don't know why Square Man came here?"

"He goes from planet to planet, one after another, getting rid of curves," said Red Eye. "He was born in the place where lines begin."

"I don't understand what that means," said Lucy.

"I read about it in my book," said Flor. "A place of great power. Every line in the entire universe begins there. He himself is made entirely of lines. He has no curves, inside or out."

"Yeah, and he's so small he has to stand up twice to cast a shadow," Lucy added.

"This can't be the end of the story," Flor said. "Dr. Pi told me this was all going to happen, and it was up to you and me, Lucy, to fix it."

"Well, I can't think of anything. Right now I feel about as helpful as a back pocket on a shirt."

"He said I had more to learn about blowing fire. I wonder if I can blow fire into something living. What would happen?"

"It would burn to bits and float away like a bunch of charred scraps of paper," said Lucy. "Or you'd cook someone to death."

"You and your crazy imagination," Flor laughed. "It's not fire like on your stove or in your fireplace. It's a kind of cosmic fire. It keeps everything alive. What would happen if I blew fire into Red Eye, for instance?"

"Don't blow it into Red Eye," said Lucy. "Blow it into me."

"Are you serious?"

"Definitely."

"And what if the fire does something weird, like blast you into a thousand fragments? I'm sure your dad would love me for that."

"Well, just blow a little, then, and see what happens. I'm not scared. I'm ready for the fire!"

Flor frowned. "The thing is, I have to call the winds of the four directions. Last time I did it, we all held hands and went around in a circle, chanting. But here I'm completely stuck in this stupid square hole."

Red Eye had been listening carefully all this time.

"How long does it take to blow this fire?" he asked.

"A minute or two," said Flor.

"I can let you out for one minute."

"You can?"

"There's a switch on the wall that releases the magnet holding your feet. But if you can't do this really fast," he warned, "I have to put you right back."

Flor gulped. She looked at Lucy. "You're sure, Pipsqueak?"

"As sure as a month of Sundays. As sure as a new boat before it gets wet. I am as sure as a bullfrog with wings. As totally and absolutely, completely and forever sure as . . ."

"Okay, okay!"

And Flor nodded to Red Eye, who clacked across the floor and quietly pulled the switch.

"You're both free now," he said.

The girls climbed out of their holes. Flor fished her magic key out of her pocket, turning a small knob and removing a tiny scroll.

"It says to light the cosmic fire, everybody must hold hands, facing outward. Red Eye and Lucy, that's you. Red Eye, be gentle with your claws, okay? Everybody ready? We've got to turn to the east, north, west, and south. We're calling the winds of the four directions. The winds will start blowing. And we have to repeat this magic phrase: *Eadem mutata resurgo semperdem.*"

"Those words are even uglier than the ones on *my* key!" Lucy protested. "They'll sound like stones in my mouth."

"They're in Latin, just like yours. And Latin is not ugly, just different."

"What do they mean?"

"They mean, 'I shall arise the same, though changed.' The fire will change you. It's like you're rising up out of your old self into a new self. And yet, you are still the same person, deep down. Anyway, the winds will blow until the fire appears. Are you both ready?"

"This is going to make me feel like an idiot," Lucy complained. "Like a goofball."

"Ready or not?"

"Well, I guess nobody else is here to see, so . . . okay. I'm ready."

"Ready," said the lobster, gently taking Flor's and Lucy's hands in each of his pincered claws.

"Ready," said Lucy.

And so they joined hands, each facing outward, repeating the strange words as they turned in a circle and called the winds of the four directions. And it was just like the first time Flor had done it—a pure, blazing happiness flowed like current from their hearts through their hands and back to their hearts. The huge marble emporium grew warm and seemed to fill with light. They danced like one creature. Round and round, faster and faster, dancing and singing, "*Eadem mutata resurgo semperdem. Eadem mutata resurgo semperdem. Eadem mutata resurgo semperdem.*"

And then the fire appeared. A small flame in the center of the circle. The flame became a heavenly fire, a pale fire, gold and white. The fire rose up in long licks. Flor let go of the others' hands. The power was in her alone now. Once again, she knew what she had to do. She turned to Lucy and blew with all her might.

LUCY CATCHES A MOST
UNUSUAL HORSE

H oly cow," Flor breathed.

"Double holy cow and add a holy wow," said Lucy, looking down upon herself from a great height. The bottom half of her body had transformed itself. Instead of two legs she had four. Instead of feet she had hooves. "I'm half horse. Look at me. All white."

She switched her tail.

"A mighty fine creature," agreed Flor, gazing up at Lucy's head. "Were you by any chance thinking about horses when I blew?"

"I'm always thinking about horses. Seeing as I'm going to be a world-famous horse rustler."

"You know you're a centaur, don't you?" Flor said.

"What's a centaur?"

"It's a legendary creature that's half horse and half human. From the hips down, you're simply all horse."

"I have this unbearable urge to gallop." She stomped on the floor. "I'm going to tear up the halls of this palace. I'm going to smash doors with these hooves."

"Ahem."

It was the lobster.

"Flor," said Red Eye.

"What?"

"Could you blow me some fire too?"

If the lobster wasn't so scaly, Flor would have said he was blushing. "Why, certainly." She hesitated. "Hold hands, everybody. And Red Eye, think hard about what you want to be most, while I blow."

A few minutes later, as Flor blew the fire at Red Eye, he shriveled up to nothing, and then out of his crumpled scales stepped a large, long-legged bird, all white, with great, enormous wings and a long, thin beak.

"My gosh. A snowy egret," said Flor.

"What's a snowy egret?" asked Lucy.

"I've seen them in Central Park in Manhattan," explained Flor. "We would take rowboats onto the lake, and watch the egrets walk like ballet dancers in the marshes."

Red Eye said, "They used to soar in the sky in the Time Before the Square. They would dive into the water to catch fish. I always wished I could be like them."

"Can I touch your feathers?" asked Flor.

He nodded.

"They're so soft. Not like scales at all."

"Yes," he said shyly.

"And your eyes? The squares are all gone. Does the world look different?"

"Very different. It's strange and wonderful."

"Sheesh, I wish I could blow fire into myself," said Flor. "But I guess nobody can do that."

Then they heard a familiar, if distant, voice.

"One, two, three, four!"

"Just in time," said Red Eye.

"Nevermore and nevermore! Hello, girls, I'm back. I gave that square chamber a little squeeze. Just a little one. Lines and angles, let's unite—"

Square Man stopped cold. He stared first at Lucy the centaur, then at the snowy egret, and finally at Flor, who was still pretty much herself, though her face was flushed with a new courage.

"Wh-what have we got here?" he stuttered.

"Transformation," said Flor.

"The end of squares," said Lucy.

"Girl power," Flor added.

"The revenge of the round," said Lucy, giggling.

Red Eye lifted into flight and soared in smooth circles around the marble emporium.

"See him fly?" said Flor. "Very un-square of him. Then again, you got rid of all the birds here, because birds don't fly in rectangles."

"They fly round and round," Lucy added. She could see Square Man was red with fury. His tiny eyes welled up with tears.

"How dare you—," spluttered Square Man. "How dare you joke about squares and circles! Laughing at me again, like they all do. I have been to two hundred planets this year alone, and slapped the Rule of the Square upon them all! And just like you, they all laughed at me first." He looked around him. "Where is Red Eye? What have you done to Red Eye?"

"He's an egret now," said Flor calmly.

Square Man stared at the white bird. "That can't be Red Eye."

"It is," said Lucy.

Square Man squinted.

"I simply don't believe it. I don't know where that bird came from."

"I am truly Red Eye, just transformed," the snowy egret said, luxuriously stretching his wings.

"Red Eye was devoted to me. He was there by my side day and night. You are a strange bird who could not possibly be my lobster."

"You thought I was devoted. I was only lost and alone," said Red Eye. "I hated every minute I served you. I hated being on dry land. You gave me no other choice. You even threatened to blind me."

"I wasn't really going to do it," said Square Man.

"Then why did you try to scare me?"

"I was afraid at first, that maybe . . . you'd run off."

"To where? You took away all the water."

Square Man shrugged and turned now to Lucy. "Rectangles?"

"Water?" she retorted.

"No. Not water. There is no water here."

"Who said we have to do it here?"

"Where do you expect to do it?"

"At the ice factory, naturally."

"The rectangles need to be here on Planet Square, where I can store them safely and use them to unwind spirals when I need to."

"No deal."

And with that, Lucy got up and stomped her forelegs, and when she stomped her forelegs, she suddenly remembered she was no longer a pipsqueak, the shortest girl in her class, the tiniest future horse rustler in the world.

She was a mythical creature.

"Let's go!" she said. "Flor, get on Red Eye's back. Red Eye, fly! Take us straight to the square chamber!"

"Nevermore!" Square Man shouted. "Nevermore! Nevermore! Nevermore!"

But they didn't stop to listen.

"All the windows will now be walls! Done! The whole place is a prison. There is no light anywhere. It's black as night. Nobody can stop me. So fly wherever you want. You are flying to your doom!"

Red Eye was soaring down long, cavernous stone halls with Flor clinging to his back.

"Who cares if the windows are walls. I know these halls by heart, Lucy," called Red Eye. "I don't need any light. Just follow me."

And Lucy did, galloping with a speed and power she had never in her life imagined she could feel. She felt the impact of the stone floor in thrilling shivers through her body each time her hooves hit the ground and lifted off it. She knew she could outrun anybody, and that no creature, wild or human, would ever be able to catch her.

CHAPTER 10

A MOST UNUSUAL DRESS

"I t's just a little setback," Lucy said.

"I don't understand," Red Eye murmured, feeling along the wall once again with his wing. "This was exactly where the square chamber was. This is where we were all standing just two hours ago."

"Could he have moved it?"

"I suppose. Squares always do his bidding."

"I hope he didn't shrink it down to nothing and—" Flor couldn't finish the thought.

"How are we going to find them?" said Lucy. "It is blacker than a crow on a moonless night."

The bird, the centaur, and the ten-year-old Brooklyn girl were silent, listening to each other breathe.

"We don't have much time," Lucy said finally. "He's going to show up again, no doubt about that."

"I'm going to stay here," said Flor, sliding down against the wall and hugging her knees. "I'm going to wait for Dr. Pi."

"What does that mean?"

"I need to be sure he's safe," she said stubbornly. "I'm going to wait here until he finds me or I find him."

"How are you going to do that?"

"I have no clue."

"We can't just leave you," Lucy said. "C'mon, Pinkie."

"I'm staying here."

"Well, sheesh."

"I know that Dr. Pi wouldn't desert me if I was stuck in a shrinking square chamber. And I'm not going to desert him, either. Because you may not understand this, but without his fire he really doesn't have a lot of wizard power. And the fire is back in his pie shop, where he always tends it. So Dr. Pi needs me."

"I can see your point," said Red Eye. "But how can he find us in the dark?"

"He probably can't. I can't even read my magic book in the dark. It's basically hopeless."

"Well, Pinkie, there's only one answer," Lucy said.

"What's that?"

"Like you said before. You should blow fire into yourself."

There was silence. Finally Flor said, "How exactly should I do that?"

"I don't know. Like maybe you take deep breaths of it. Make it go into you and change you. See what happens."

"I don't think it's possible," Flor said, but there was a tinge of hope in her voice.

"Can't hurt to try, can it?"

"But all I've ever wanted to be is a fashion designer," said Flor. "What will the cosmic fire do about that?"

Lucy thought for a moment. "Well, like Dad says, sometimes you just have to go around your elbow to get to your thumb."

"What does *that* mean?"

"My thumb is right here, see? I shouldn't have to go

back around my elbow to get to it. It means sometimes things get complicated or a little tough, but as long as you get to your thumb eventually, that's what counts."

"I like that saying," said Red Eye.

"But you don't have an elbow," Lucy pointed out.

"Sometimes you have to go around your wing to get to your leg," said Red Eye, flapping his gorgeous white wings and lifting one long leg.

"Or go around your knee to get to your toe," said Flor.

"You have to go around your head to get to your heart," said Red Eye.

"That's a good one!" said Flor. "Okay, I'm willing to give this crazy idea a try. Shall we?"

Red Eye offered a wing to both girls, who joined hands and once again called the winds that brought the fire. But this time, when Flor felt the flames rising within her, she held her breath and scrunched her eyes closed and imagined the fire filling her body, from head to toe.

She could feel the fire hesitating, as if it had never done this before.

Fire, she asked it silently, *please. Blow into me. Change me.*

It circled around inside her, as if looking for a place to go. And then suddenly, when she couldn't hold her breath any longer, it leaped outside of her.

But it did not leave her.

It draped itself along her body, a skirt of fire, a shirt of fire, sleeves of fire. She blazed with pale light.

"Well, Miss Fashion Guru," said Lucy. "You've really done it this time. I think you have a dress of fire now."

"I do," said Flor in wonder. She lifted her arms and the fire followed, in long, liquid flames. A dress of fire that shifted with her every movement, and didn't burn.

"Hey, girl, you're cosmic," Lucy joked. "Are you going to put this in your New York collection?"

Flor laughed. "No way."

"It's bright as a fresh spring morning in here," said Red Eye. "We can find the door to the square chamber now. Just look for a red iron door. It's only a question of which hall it's in."

"How many halls are there?" asked Flor.

"One hundred and thirty-four."

"You've got to be kidding," said Lucy. "Who needs all

those hallways? You know what? He has a worse complex about being small than I ever did."

"You made up for being a pipsqueak with your big personality," Flor said.

"Square Man thinks everybody hates him," said Lucy. "Except Red Eye, of course. I think he had no clue what he was doing to Red Eye. He convinced himself he actually had one friend, but otherwise, he's got to take revenge on everyone."

"Sometimes when I couldn't sleep," said Red Eye, "I would just lie there with my eyes closed. And I would hear him talking to himself."

"What would he say?"

"He would kind of argue with himself. Like he had two personalities. One would start out pleading. 'I am sure I was born for a reason. There's nothing wrong with being small and square. If the universe created me, then I am good, like all creation. There's a place for me somewhere to be happy. Where people will like me. Where they'd give me half a chance.' And then this other voice would come out of him, like he was just shutting himself up.

'You're a mistake. Nobody will ever accept you. You look weird and you act weird. So don't even think about trying. The only answer is to conquer all.'"

"Hmmm."

"So what next?" asked Lucy.

"Let me check my book. It always helps me when I don't know what to do. And I can read by the light of my own dress."

Flor unclasped her white purse and pulled out the book, turning to the last page. And she began to read out loud:

"Before Square Man left the chamber, he said to Dr. Pi and Buddy Moon, 'I'm going to shut you in now and shrink this chamber. It's going to get hot and uncomfortable for you two. You'll be pressed together like sardines in a can.' He waited for a response, but the wizard simply smiled benignly, and Buddy Moon simply nodded. Square Man shook his head in disbelief. 'And this is the reaction of the two great guardians of the Spiral and the Golden Rectangle? Just nodding and smiling?' Dr. Pi answered quietly, 'The girls are destined to solve this, not us, and all that is good and balanced in this universe wants it that way.'

"'Sounds like you're admitting defeat, that's all,' said Square Man, before he shut the door. Then he said, "*Divina sectia, divina sectia,* hide yourself now. There shall be no visible door, no crack, no evidence of the square chamber. And shrink to two-thirds of your present size. In half an hour, shrink to half.'

"The chamber shrunk, and the door disappeared from sight. Only one key could open the door now—the key owned by Lucy Moon. But she could only find the lock by tuning into her heart. Love would guide the key to the invisible lock."

Flor turned to Lucy. "Well, Pip, it's all up to you now."

Lucy fished for her key. "It's not hard to feel love in my heart," she said. "I only have to think of Daddy and Nell."

She closed her eyes and thought of her dad, with the crinkles in the corners of his eyes, and his wavy brown hair streaked with silver, and his favorite old sneakers that he wore to work every day. She thought of Nell on her wedding day, her face aglow with joy, as Matt carried her over the threshold of the front door and down steps blanketed in billows of snow. She thought of how the family watched TV at night, Nell on one side of the sofa, her dad on the other, and Lucy stretched out between them.

And the key practically yanked her three feet to the left, and almost pulled her hand to the stone. She saw nothing there, but when she pushed it, it went right in. She turned the key. The door opened.

Her dad was there, sitting scrunched over with his knees to his chest so his head wouldn't bump the ceiling.

"Thank you for rescuing me, Pip," he said with a grin, and crawled out of the chamber on his hands and knees. "And by the way, being half horse looks good on you."

"I love it," said Lucy. ""Flor blew fire into me, and I turned into a centaur. That's what she calls it. A centaur."

"I know what a centaur is," he said, smiling.

"Although I don't know if I want to look like this when I go back home."

"Mr. Moon," said Flor. "Where is Dr. Pi?"

"I don't exactly know," said Buddy, "but I expect he's somewhere in here."

"I don't see him anywhere," said Flor.

"As soon as Square Man shut us in," Buddy said, "Dr. Pi told me to stand in the corner, and he began to do back flips. It was really something to see, with that jolly belly. I had no idea he was such a nimble athlete."

"He's got a belly from all those pies he eats," said Flor. "Did he get smaller and smaller?"

"Yup. Each time he did a back flip, he got smaller, until he completely disappeared. I think he figured soon enough there would only be room for one of us. Which is the case, as you can see."

"Oh, thank goodness," Flor breathed, and gave a big grin. "He's safe, then. I've seen him do that before. It's part of the power of the Spiral. He can make himself as small or big as he wants. He just spun himself small. He's in there somewhere. Probably floating up in the corner like a speck of dust."

Suddenly a small blue and red marble rolled out of the chamber. It rolled down the hall, and as it rolled, it grew bigger and bigger, until it became a belly, and arms, legs, and a head.

"Dr. Pi!" Flor shouted in relief, running to him.

"My, you're lovely, all decked out in cosmic fire," he said.

"You still have some magic left," she said. "I'm so relieved."

"I always have a bit of magic up my sleeve," he said. "That will never change."

Then they heard a familiar voice.

"One, two, three, four, " said Square Man, marching down the hall.

He stopped.

"Unbelievable. You people are so annoying. I won't ask how you managed to trick me again." He walked up to Flor. "What's with your new dress?"

"Do you like it?" She lifted her arms, and he watched the flames rise and fall.

"Fire becomes her," said Dr. Pi. "Literally."

"It's very nice. I'm wondering about the purse, though. At first I assumed it was a fashion accessory. But it doesn't match your new outfit at all, and you've kept it anyway. May I have a look? I should have had a look before."

"No way."

"I'm a gentleman. So I'll grab it."

"You won't take it," said Red Eye, swooping down and snatching the purse in his beak.

"Come back here!" demanded Square Man.

But Red Eye began to soar down the long hall.

"Oh, phooey! I didn't want to hurt anybody," said Square Man, snapping his fingers three times quickly. "A wall appears!"

Suddenly, just as Red Eye turned the corner, he smashed into a wall and fell. The purse fell from his beak, and the key rolled out.

"Had to place a wall in the hall," said Square Man, leaping nimbly over to the injured bird and grabbing the key. "Looks like you broke your wing. Oh well. Your friends will tend to you."

He looked at the group.

"Girls and their keys. Whatever you've been doing, Flor, you won't be doing it anymore. I have your key. I suspect this will finally turn the tables on all of you. At some point Lucy will decide to make me rectangles. Until then, sorry to say, I have to have another wall in the hall."

As he left, a wall rose up behind him, and they found themselves in what amounted to a long, rectangular room.

"We're trapped inside another golden rectangle," sighed Buddy.

"But I still have *my* key," Lucy said.

"And I still have my book," said Flor, retrieving her purse from the floor and snapping the clasp shut.

"Flor," said Dr. Pi.

"Yes?"

"You can blow fire without the key. The key simply contains the secret instructions, meant only for the key holder. The problem is, if Square Man figures out how to open it and reads the scroll, then he will be able to blow fire too. And I expect him to figure it out sooner or later. He's a clever little man. It's just that he's a thief. I have a feeling he stole most of his powers."

"We need to get it back from him. Or he really might win, right, Dr. Pi?" asked Flor.

"He might," said Dr. Pi sadly. "And that's not a good thing, given that he's a four-inch person who wants to rule the universe."

"Let's have a look at that wing," said Buddy, walking over to Red Eye and testing it gently. "I've rescued many a baby bird that fell out of its nest, and more than a few the cat went after. Does it hurt?"

"Not much," said Red Eye bravely.

Buddy lifted and pressed it gently. Red Eye made a bird whimper.

"You won't be able to fly for a few weeks," said Buddy, "but you'll be okay. For now, you'll have to walk like the rest of us two-leggeds."

"So. Exactly how do we get out of here?" asked Flor.

"It's not that hard," said Dr. Pi. "I've been wanting to show you this for years, and now the time is right."

"I think I know what you're going to say," said Buddy with a sparkle in his eye.

"Truly. We're in a golden rectangle. And so, right here, in this rectangle, is the curve of the invisible spiral. Which you can't see, and neither can I, but I can calculate easily from any golden rectangle."

"How's that?" asked Lucy.

"It has to do with the square inside the golden rectangle.

Every golden rectangle can be divided into a square and another, smaller golden rectangle. Don't worry. It's second nature to me."

"And then what do we do?" asked Lucy.

"We just step onto the spiral. And walk on it."

"Well, if that don't beat the band," she marveled. "Walking on a spiral you can't see and never knew was there."

"The spiral will lead us out. The rectangle offers up the spiral. It's the law of the universe. In fact, I might go so far as to say that the rectangle becomes the spiral. The only concern is, I don't know where we'll end up. We might just keep walking the spiral right into outer space!"

CHAPTER 11

RECTANGLES GALORE

The first thing Dr. Pi did was measure the length and width of the hallway, using his feet as a ruler. "At my full height my feet are exactly twelve inches long," he explained with a laugh. Then he did various calculations in his head, murmuring every so often. "One, two, five . . . three hundred . . . forty-seven . . ."

After a few minutes he nodded. "I've got it," he said. "Follow me."

What happened next looked like magic. He went to a spot on the floor and stepped up into the air.

"It's there," he announced. "Like a very thin wire. Quite wonderful."

Very slowly, continuing to check his calculations, and

jiggling and wiggling with his arms out to keep his balance, he went up an invisible curve.

"Follow me," he said, pausing near the ceiling.

"Dr. Pi, you look like a very bad circus act," said Buddy, laughing. "Well, I always wanted to join the circus. I'll follow on faith."

He stepped easily onto the invisible spiral, and walked around and up. "Look at that," said Lucy in wonder. The ceiling simply opened up, and Dr. Pi squeezed through the opening, grunting.

"Come on, girls," said Buddy. "And Red Eye."

Red Eye hesitated. "Does anybody mind if I stay here?"

"The wing really hurts?" Buddy asked.

Red Eye nodded.

"You should rest, then. We'll come back for you once the girls have saved the day."

Lucy ran to the spot, felt for the spiral, and turned to Flor.

"You can't see it, but it's right there."

She held her hand out to Flor, who took it.

"I've been here before, sort of," Flor said to Lucy as they felt their way up the spiral curve.

"What do you mean?"

"I met the Spirit of the Spiral. It sounds goofy, I know, but I really did. She took me through the Milky Way, and even into this spiral bone that's inside your ear. She showed me all these spiral forms in nature. That was after I just stepped out into outer space, like—"

"This?" Lucy breathed as they exited the palace and walked up the curve into the night air. "Wow. I wonder if there's a spiral like this in my hay rectangle, and in all Daddy's ice containers?"

"There must be."

"Wild," said Lucy. "It's like a secret trapdoor that's all over the place and nobody knows about."

"But the thing is—if you just try to jump off, do you fall through space, or do you end up back in the rectangle? Don't let go of my hand!"

"No way, Miss Pinkie Cosmic Fire—if we fall, we fall together."

"Speaking of which, I wonder if I can ever take off this

dress? I don't think I can go to school dressed in fire."

The girls had caught up to the others.

"Now," Dr. Pi said, "as we cross outside the golden rectangle, we will pass through a bigger square, and a bigger golden rectangle. When the spiral intersects with the next rectangle, we can jump off, if we wish."

With that, he stepped off the curve and disappeared. They followed, and soon found themselves in a long rectangle with shiny polished wood floors and two deep gutters on either side.

A large, hard black ball was hurtling toward them at incredible speed. They scattered as it smashed past them and turned to watch it barrel onward and crash into three huge, odd-shaped white pegs.

"Gad night a livin'," said Lucy. "We're in a bowling alley!"

All three pins went down, and there was loud applause. Then a voice called, "What's going on with those other pins? I see four new pins popped up—and they are really strange! One looks like a horse and another looks like a burning girl!"

"Extra pins. That's not in the rules," said a second voice. "What the heck. Roll another ball and smash 'em down!"

"I don't think we want to linger here," said Dr. Pi. "Shall we be on our way as fast as we can?"

They climbed back onto the spiral and walked into space, just in time to miss another bowling ball.

The next rectangle was unbelievably soft and white and perfumed. At the edges it had blue embroidery.

"Ahhh," said Buddy, "I know what this is." He turned to Lucy. "Your mom had one of these. It's an old-fashioned tissue box. The tissues are the finest linen and hand-embroidered."

"And we all fit into it? How is that? These handkerchiefs must belong to a giant," said Lucy.

They left, and landed on a graham cracker of sorts. Dr. Pi broke off a piece to discover roasted marshmallow and chocolate inside. "Interesting," he said, tasting it. "Perhaps I'll make a pie like this when I get back."

"You don't know what a s'more is, Dr. Pi?" asked Lucy. He shook his head.

"I guess you've never sat around a campfire. You stick your marshmallow on a skewer, hold it over the fire until it's roasted, and put it between two graham crackers with a piece of chocolate. And that's a s'more. We have a fire pit in our backyard and make 'em all the time."

"I adore a s'more," said Dr. Pi, laughing. "I guess I can't eat all of it, or we'll have nothing to stand on."

At the next place they landed they paused.

Flor said, "A parking lot with about five hundred parking spaces. All rectangles, of course."

"Like a deserted Walmart at night," said Lucy. "This is cool and all, but we could travel through galactic rectangles forever. Shouldn't we get back to Planet Square?"

"How do we do *that*?" asked Flor.

"Maybe I should do the rectangle dance," said Lucy.

"The rectangle dance?" Dr. Pi asked.

"Like I did in the barn, like the key told me to. I was walking in a rectangle and chanting those magic words. *Divina sectia.* The rectangle just lifted me out of Puddleville and dumped me in Flor's closet like it had a mind of its own. Remember you even said it had saved me?"

"Rectangles do have some funny ideas sometimes," said Buddy.

"They do, Daddy?"

"My blocks of ice have done some mighty strange things in their day. I've seen a block of ice waiting for a truck that needs it and is caught in traffic and running late. . . . I've seen that ice stay completely frozen in the summer sun. Without melting at all. That's not possible."

"So then I definitely should do the rectangle dance," said Lucy. "Flor, do it with me. Okay?"

Flor swallowed hard. "Okay, sure."

"And no matter what, don't let go of my hand?"

"Right."

"And if it works—well, you guys follow us. Just do the same as you see me do. We'll pray the rectangle delivers us all to the same place."

But sadly, it did not. The Golden Rectangle had a plan of its own.

A LONELY SQUARE

Square Man was alone, as he usually was. He was tired. Usually right about now he would turn to Red Eye, who would be dozing a few feet away. And he'd talk to the lobster.

"I thought he liked me," Square Man fretted. "But I guess not."

It used to be fun, arriving on a new planet, and surprising everyone with his magnificent powers despite his small size. He used to enjoy watching them gape, and tremble with fear. It used to be thrilling, seeing all the circles unwind into lines. He had felt so good, replacing round things with square things. He'd leave the planet with a sense of symmetry, a job well done.

But it didn't feel good anymore. He was tired of fighting

Lucy and Flor. He couldn't even get a rise out of Buddy Moon and Dr. Pi. They seemed unfazed by him.

"There's a reason I was born," he said to himself as he often did. "I belong in this universe just like everybody else. I'm square, and my mission is to convert every planet I can to the Way of the Square." Then he paused, and in another voice he scolded himself, "Nobody cares. Nobody loves a square like you do."

He sighed and got to his feet. Time to check on the girls. When he arrived at the wall he'd placed, he snapped his fingers once again and it melted away.

"So, Lucy Moon," he said triumphantly, "now we will come to terms."

But no one answered.

"Nobody's here," said Square Man, looking around. "Except a snowy egret that seems fast asleep and probably ate Red Eye alive."

The bird stirred and opened its eyes.

"It's not possible!" said Square Man. He marched up to Red Eye. "Where have they gone?"

"Up the spiral," said Red Eye, and he said nothing

more. He simply closed his eyes and went back to sleep.

"Wake up," Square Man said, shaking the bird frantically by his good, uninjured wing.

"What do you want?" said the egret. "They found the spiral in the rectangle and walked out. I saw it with my very eyes. A bird's eyes. Not a lobster's eyes."

"It's not possible," said Square Man. "Now I have no idea where they've gone! They could have climbed a hundred spirals by now! They could be gone forever."

"True." Red Eye hesitated. "But I don't really think so. They'll be back for me. They said they would, and I believe them. They're that kind of folk. Good folk. True to their word."

Square Man was silent. Then he looked at Red Eye. "You don't look half-bad as a bird."

"Thank you."

"I don't know why you betrayed me. I fed you and housed you and treated you well."

"But it was what you wanted, not what I wanted, don't you see?"

"I suppose," the tiny man said reluctantly. "Well, just for tonight, keep me company, for old times' sake."

"You can stay here if it gives you comfort," said Red Eye. "But I don't have anything to say, and I'm going back to sleep."

A POOL OF TEARS

Where in the good Lord's creation are we?" whispered Lucy. "Where did the rectangle dance put us?"

Flor held her friend's hand fast. "I don't know," she whispered back.

"It looks like a big construction site," said Lucy. "Like somebody started building a planet and just left all the stuff heaped everywhere and went away."

Indeed, all around them were piles of beams, bricks, spools of thick wire, and large, jutting pieces of glass.

"Let's walk a little," suggested Flor.

They picked their way carefully among the mess, climbing over stacked wood and metal rods.

"We're completely lost," said Flor.

"There must be a reason we're here," said Lucy.

"Look, there's a clearing."

"That's a lake."

They approached the lake slowly, looking around. Finally they sat down at the base of a large, blue hill.

Then the biggest raindrop Flor and Lucy had ever seen fell, *kerplunk*, in the middle of the lake.

"I don't understand why it's raining," said Lucy. "There's not a single cloud in the sky."

Another large drop fell, and it was followed by a sob. And a loud sniffle.

The girls looked up.

"Yuck!" cried Flor. A drop had fallen directly on her face. "Where is this rain coming from?"

The hill they were leaning against moved.

The girls ran.

"Stop!" a voice cried. "Don't run. Please don't run . . . why . . . it's two little girls. I've been alone here for so long. I am in desperate need of company. It's just that . . ."

A huge face peered down at them. "You're so very tiny . . . why . . . you're both barely a few inches tall."

Flor craned her neck back as far as it would go and looked up.

"It's a giant. I think it's a woman. And she's so big . . . so big . . ."

"It looks like one of you is on fire?" the giant said. "I've cried a pool of tears here, which is now a lake, since I've been crying ever since everything got ruined. You can jump into my pool of tears and put that fire out if you like."

"No," said Flor. "It's a cosmic fire, not a hot fire. I'm fine. And it's my dress anyway."

"Where are we?" asked Lucy. "Is this a planet of giants? Is that why you're so big?"

"I'm a perfectly normal size," the giant replied. "It's you two who are so terribly small. But I don't mean that as an insult. You're both very adorable, now that I've gotten a good look at you. Especially the little one with hooves. You're charming, really."

"Thank you," said Lucy. "I haven't had hooves that long, actually. We've clearly ended up on the wrong planet. We'll have to do the rectangle dance again. There's no sign of Square Man here."

"Did you say Square Man?" the giant said.

The girls nodded.

The giant began to cry again.

"He has ruined my life . . . and ruined my planet . . . do you know him?"

"Oh yeah, we know him," said Lucy. "He's as low as a toad in a dry well. He's trying to destroy our planet too."

"Oh, that's terrible," the giant said. "Where are you two girls from?"

"Planet Earth," said Flor.

"Planet Earth! Are you really from planet Earth?"

"Yes," said Lucy. "Is that such a big deal?"

"I've heard about planet Earth. Everyone learns about planet Earth in grade school. It's supposed to be a very beautiful planet, with ice caps on either end, and blue water, and fertile land. And it's a place where everything gets along, right? All the rectangles and squares and circles and spirals and triangles . . . they all have a chance to express themselves there. Am I right?"

"Well," said Flor, "I guess so. I never thought about it that way."

"This was a planet of angles. They just weren't right angles. More like triangles, and trapezoids, and pentagrams. Just anything with an angle. It was really a nice place, though. I built it all myself. I had many visitors come and admire it. Until Square Man came and destroyed everything." The giant sighed. "So sit down, girls. Relax on the shore of my pool of tears."

"Thank you, giant," said Lucy. "We'd love to, but we have to be on our way now. We still have a chance to save planet Earth."

"If two men show up here, a wizard and an ice maker, tell them we were here and left. Okay?" Flor added.

"I hope they visit soon." The giant began to cry again. "I'm so lonely, and my planet is ugly now. Nobody comes to see me anymore because there is nothing left to see."

"Well, if we can fix it, you can rebuild your planet," said Flor. "Have faith."

"We've got to go," said Lucy.

And they said good-bye to the giant, joined hands, did the rectangle dance, and fell into a new world.

FIRE IN THE HEART

This new world was on fire.

Tongues of flame leaped up eagerly, licking and lapping everything they burned. Sparks flew, and new fires burst into being.

The light was blindingly beautiful.

"It hurts," whispered Lucy.

"Really?" said Flor. The fire did not touch her but seemed to bow before her, gently lick her hair, and move on. Her dress of fire met the fire around her, and it was as if they were old friends.

"How does it hurt? Is it hot?" she asked Lucy.

"No . . . not hot . . . it's just . . . too much. I feel like I'm going to shatter. It's too much energy."

"Here, hold my hand," said Flor. "Do you feel better now?"

Lucy breathed in relief. "Yes. It's like you're protecting me. Thanks."

Flor looked around her and could see nothing but flame. "I wonder where we are?"

"Who could tell? The fire has already burned up everything."

"Wait—there's something moving." She squinted. "I think it's some little animal, maybe a hamster or mouse, running toward us."

The little creature kept running toward them, and now Flor could see it throwing out its hands and crying, "What have I done? What have I done? I had no idea! It was just an experiment! And now I have burned up my own planet! Owww! Owww! It's too strong! It's too bright! How do I stop this fire? If only I had water! Help me! Help me! Somebody help me!"

"Oh my gosh," said Flor. "You would not believe it, Pip, but that's Square Man."

"He must have opened your key, Pinkie, and followed the instructions on the scroll."

"But he seems to have overdone it somehow."

Square Man saw the two girls and skidded to a stop. "Flor! Lucy! Thank goodness you're here, my dear old friends! I'm alone here! Except for Red Eye—I mean, the white bird—whatever it is. Flor, stop this fire immediately, please. I don't know how it started!"

"Oh, you definitely know how it got started," she said. "And why should I stop it?"

"To save us! Me and Red Eye, and my home, and everything I own and worked so hard for!" he shouted. "My palace is next!"

"You destroy worlds, and I should save yours. Hmmm. That doesn't make a lot of sense, does it? Anyway, give me my key. You stole it, and you clearly opened it and tried to blow the cosmic fire."

"I don't have any key," he protested, panting.

Flor shrugged and turned to Lucy.

"Pipsqueak," said Flor, "can you endure the energy of the fire on your own for a few minutes?"

"Yes," said Lucy bravely.

Flor started to walk to the Square Palace.

"Where are you going?" asked Square Man.

"To save Red Eye."

"No—I mean—okay, but—can't you just put out the fire?"

"I don't know."

"Here," he said, throwing her key at her. "Here's your silly old key. I don't want it anyway, if it starts fires like this. I feel like I'm going to fly into a thousand pieces. It's like some kind of horrible lightning storm!"

Flor took the key.

Lucy was shivering from the heat. Her teeth were clattering, and her hands were shaking.

"Look at your friend!" he said to Flor. "How can you let her suffer so?"

"I'm okay," said Lucy, wincing.

"Before I do anything at all to help you," said Flor, "you must give me the wand."

"The wand?" repeated the little man. "What wand?"

"You know exactly what wand I'm talking about."

"I have no clue."

"The wand you stole from the place where all beginnings begin."

He was silent, stunned.

"Absolutely not," he fumed. "I'm not giving up the wand. I'd rather burn to death."

"Then burn up in the cosmic fire," said Flor. "Let it all burn and cleanse everything and return it to pure energy. It's already getting a little intense in here, isn't it? Lucy, hold my hand again. Let's go."

Lucy took her hand and instantly stopped shivering. "Gad night a livin'," she breathed. "What an awesome relief."

"Hold my hand too!" cried Square Man, running after them.

The fire unfurled in a massive wave of orange with blue at the very tips of the many flames. It roared toward them in a glorious blaze. Flor walked ahead, unafraid. She met the fire, and it seemed to bow and separate and move on. She walked up to the palace, and the doors swung open, and she walked down the hall to find Red Eye.

Square Man ran behind them, crying out in pain.

The fire consumed everything in its path.

Flor stopped, and Lucy stopped with her. "This is the hallway," Flor said. "There's no sign of Red Eye."

"He must have flown off," said Lucy.

"You think so?"

"Sure. Wouldn't you if you were a bird and the world was burning up?"

"I guess he's okay, then."

She turned around and faced Square Man.

"The fire is going to eat you alive. You're going to turn back into energy soon. Is that really what you want?"

"I can't give up my magic wand," he sobbed like a little child. "It's my everything."

Square Man's tiny face was flushed. He lay down on the ground.

"No," he said, breathing heavily. "No."

Something strange happened to Flor then. She didn't feel sorry for Square Man, really, but suddenly she felt as if she understood him. He no longer seemed evil or vicious. It was as if the fire had imparted some kind of wisdom, some ability to see past the obvious.

She let go of Lucy's hand for a moment and knelt beside him.

"None of this was necessary," she said.

"What," he muttered, rolling on the ground in agony.

"Turning planet after planet into squares as revenge. The round people were mean, but that's the way people are when they see something different. They don't understand, and sometimes they laugh, and sometimes they're even really nasty about it, just because somebody looks a little different. But there is a place for you, where you can be happy."

"No," he moaned.

"You just have no faith. Why, you'd be perfectly acceptable on planet Earth. Scientists would be fascinated by you. I could design some square clothes. You might like New York. It's full of oddballs. And there are lots of tall, rectangular buildings there."

"No," he said. "No, no, no. My magic wand is everything to me. I'd rather die."

She sighed. "Okay. Lucy, let's do the rectangle dance. It's time to get out of here."

Square Man watched them from the ground as Flor followed Lucy, tracing a rectangle and chanting the magic words, "*Divina sectia.*"

And at the very last moment he reached out his hand. "Take me with you."

Flor stopped. "The wand, please."

He handed it over. He had never looked so pitiful. His head hung. "It's all over now," he said.

"No," said Flor, "it's all just begun."

She grabbed Square Man's hand, even as they all fell out of Planet Square and into a new world.

HOME AT LAST

Where are we?" asked Square Man. "Why am I still burning up?"

They had landed in a cavernous room with hundreds of rubber rectangles laid side by side on the floor.

"We're at the ice factory," said Lucy. "And look—there's Daddy at the other end."

"And Dr. Pi," added Flor. "They got here ahead of us."

"But something's wrong," said Lucy. "Daddy looks very upset."

"And Dr. Pi is waving his hands around."

"And I'm still burning up!" shouted Square Man. "Look at me! I'm still on fire! While you two—you have gone back to being regular girls."

Flor looked down at herself. The dress of fire was gone. She looked at Lucy, who was no longer half horse.

"Oh well," said Lucy. "I don't think a centaur would have gone over well in Puddleville anyway."

She started to trot across the floor, then realized she could no longer trot.

Two legs felt kind of weird.

Buddy was walking toward them. "All my ice has melted," he said. "It's just cold water. It won't freeze, no matter what I do."

Dr. Pi was following. "It's extraordinary. This defies the laws of physics."

"I've got the saline solution down to zero degrees, and the rectangles won't freeze. I told you rectangles have a mind of their own sometimes. Well, all mine have decided to remain water until further notice."

"Water, water, water!" said Square Man excitedly. "That's exactly what I need! Please, let me dunk myself. Please!"

Buddy looked at the tiny man, who was immersed in flames.

"Ah," he said. "Maybe they have been waiting for you. Let me move one of the rubber mats. Pip, can you help me?"

Lucy knelt and moved a mat aside. Square Man went eagerly to the edge and looked down.

"Can I dive in?"

"Be my guest," said Buddy.

They all watched as he jumped into the water and began to splash around.

"How does it feel?" asked Dr. Pi.

"So good I can't tell you. But my head is still on fire. I'm going underwater."

And with that, he tumbled down into the water until he could no longer be seen.

"Now what?" Flor asked.

"Now," said Buddy, "I expect we'll have ice. Have a look."

Flor knelt down and touched the top of the water.

"It's frozen fast."

"And so is Square Man," said Buddy.

"They've all become ice," said Dr. Pi. He sighed with relief. "The world is in order again."

"Except for the wand," said Flor, holding it out to Dr. Pi. "Will you return it?"

"Yes. I'll notify the guardians of points and lines. They will restore all the planets to their original shapes."

"The spell has been broken," said Buddy.

"The spirals are safe," said Dr. Pi.

"There's a giant we should help," Lucy reminded Flor.

"That's right. Dr. Pi—will you tell the guardians, when you give them the wand, to go help the giant who built a planet of triangles?"

"Why, certainly."

"And there's one more thing."

"What's that?"

"Well," said Flor, "when I was standing in the middle of the fire, and I was safe, it was like the light of the fire showed me the truth. And the truth is that Square Man doesn't think anybody will ever like him. I know he's made a lot of trouble, a whole lot of trouble, but I swear I could feel the fire telling me to give him a chance. Maybe we should give him a chance here on Earth. I mean, without his magic wand, what can he do that's so bad anyway?"

"Not much," Dr. Pi admitted. "Still, he tried to destroy the Spiral."

"You've got a big heart, little Flor," said Buddy. "Well, let's lift the rectangle up, and push the ice out, and have a look."

He lowered a hook on a chain and fastened it onto the steel rectangle. And slowly he cranked the rectangle up and out of the floor. He maneuvered it to a dry spot, and then he pushed the block of ice out into the light.

There in the middle was the tiny man, his mouth open wide, his arms flung out, his face full of terror. Frozen fast, like a fly in a Popsicle.

"Oh sheesh," said Lucy. "We can't leave him like that, can we?"

Flor shook her head.

"Daddy," said Lucy, "melt it, please."

Buddy looked around. "Are we in agreement?"

Everybody nodded.

"Help me roll the ice outside, then."

Together they slowly pushed the large block of ice out of the factory and onto the deck in the sun, where it very slowly began to melt. Rivulets of water ran down the sides. It melted evenly, slowly growing smaller and smaller.

"It retains its golden shape," said Dr. Pi, "to the very last."

"That it does," said Buddy.

As the ice melted, Square Man looked as if he was slowly floating downward. At last he was enclosed in a rectangle of ice only slightly bigger than himself.

Finally one hand popped out of the ice.

Then the other hand popped out.

The top of his head emerged, drops of water sliding down his ears.

As soon as his face was free, he yelped and gulped for air. And then he spluttered to a stop. The ice was entirely gone, and he was standing in water. He shook himself like a dog after a heavy rain, droplets flying out in all directions.

The sun beat down, a breeze swayed the pecan trees, and a butterfly landed briefly on Square Man's head, opening and closing its golden wings, then flew off.

"You could have let me freeze forever," he said. "Why did you save me?"

"We thought maybe you would have a change of heart."

"You don't hate me? Totally and completely hate me?"

Flor shook her head.

"I have a lot of people to apologize to, don't I?" said Square Man.

"A lot."

"A lot of squares need to be turned back to circles."

"The guardians of the line will do that for you."

"I don't know how to begin a new life," he said.

"I could use your help making ice. I need an assistant," said Buddy.

"Do you really mean it?" whispered Square Man. "You really want me to stick around?"

"We do," said Buddy. "The world needs squares, just not *all* squares. And you need to learn that there is something more powerful than a circle or a square, than a rectangle or even a spiral."

"What's that?"

"Love, of course," said Buddy. "What say you all we go back to the house and eat some leftover wedding cake? It's been a long, strange day, but it all seems to have turned out all right, and a little celebration is in order."

CHAPTER 16

RED EYE IN THE SKY
WITH DIAMONDS

Lucy and Flor were in the hayloft, having a sleepover. They'd stuffed themselves with wedding cake, and then Flor had called her mother to tell her she was safe, just a thousand miles away in Georgia. "When I get home," she had promised her mother, who had been quite upset, "you can ground me forever. I'll clean the dishes after dinner every night, and I'll even scoop out the cat litter. I'll do whatever you ask, I promise!"

Then Buddy had put two sleeping bags, a few pillows, and a battery-operated fan up in the golden rectangle of hay.

It was around ten o'clock. They were staring up at the night sky through the large, open window in the loft.

"It's gorgeous. You never see stars like this in Brooklyn," said Flor. "There are too many city lights."

"We were near some of those stars just a few hours ago," said Lucy. "Nobody will ever believe it, will they?"

"Nope."

They were silent for a while.

"Hey, look up there, past that tree branch," said Lucy. "See that sprinkle of stars there?"

"I think so. Why?"

"Don't they sort of look like the shape of a lobster?"

Flor squinted. "That could be a lobster. You think it's Red Eye? That he's saying hello from a distant star somehow?"

"I don't know. Well, if it's not a lobster, it's definitely an egret," said Lucy. "Definitely, those stars there by that branch of that tree, are either a lobster or a bird."

They laughed. And then they were silent again.

"Pip?" asked Flor.

"Yeah?"

"Are you going to come visit me in Brooklyn—I mean, the regular way? Not arriving in my closet."

"You mean, like, ride me a baby alligator all the way to New York?"

"Exactly," laughed Flor. "Arrive on an alligator. My mom will love that."

"Can Nell and Matt come too?"

"Sure, why not?"

"Sounds like fun."

And once more they were silent.

"Pinkie, you got your key?" asked Lucy.

"Yep. You got yours?"

"Right in my pocket."

"That's good."

"Hey," said Lucy.

"What?"

"Do you mind if I just close my eyes and check my eyelids for holes?"

"Nope, go right ahead. That sounds like fun. I'll check mine, too."

And Lucy closed her eyes, and Flor closed hers, too.

"No holes," said Lucy contentedly.

"No holes here, either," said Flor.

And before they knew it, they were fast asleep in a bed of hay.

Inside the house Dr. Pi was snoring happily in a soft leather chair.

Square Man had climbed into the Kleenex box, stretched out on the soft tissues, and nodded off.

Buddy quietly turned off the lights and went upstairs. All was well in the world. The Golden Rectangle and the Spiral were in balance. He stood at his window for a few moments before going to bed. Up in the night sky the constellation now known as Red Eye sparkled.

Buddy Moon waved. And then he lay down like the others to sleep.